BAD DIRT

Bad Dirt

WYOMING STORIES 2

ANNIE PROULX

Xnas 2004 —
Pamela sent, opened
for bedtime reading X-mas eve —
perfect — with love from drils

FOURTH ESTATE • London and New York

First published in Great Britain in 2004 by
Fourth Estate
An imprint of HarperCollins*Publishers*
77–85 Fulham Palace Road
London W6 8JB

www.4thestate.com

Originally published in the USA in 2004 by Scribner
Copyright © Dead Line, Ltd. 2004

1

The right of Annie Proulx to be identified as the author
of this work has been asserted by her in accordance
with the Copyright, Designs and Patents Act 1988

A catalogue record for this book is available from the British Library

ISBN 0-00-719691-1

'The Trickle Down Effect', 'What Kind of Furniture Would Jesus Pick?',
'Man Crawling Out of Trees' and 'Summer of the Hot Tubs' previously
appeared in *The New Yorker*; 'The Old Badger Game' in *Playboy*;
'The Contest' in *The Virginia Quarterly Review*; and 'The Wamsutter
Wolf' in *The Paris Review*.

Designed by Erich Hobbing
Typeset in Bembo
Printed in Great Britain by
Clays Ltd, St Ives plc

For Muffy, Jon, Gail, Gillis, and Morgan

Contents

Acknowledgments

FOR HELP WITH INFORMATION ON BUFFALO BILL'S LOST film, *The Indian Wars Refought,* thanks to Assistant Archivist Anne M. Guzzo at the American Heritage Center, University of Wyoming; to Frances B. Clymer, Librarian at the McCracken Research Library of the Buffalo Bill Historical Center in Cody; to the painter David Bradley of Santa Fe, who takes an interest in the subject; and to the film industry people Linda Goldstein-Knowlton and Don Knowlton of Los Angeles. Ron Lockwood of Wyoming Game & Fish was most helpful with information about some of the department's fieldwork and for details on laws, arrest procedures, wildlife violations, and wildlife. A variety of ranchers, ranch hands, conservationists, archaeologists, and travelers also helped, and as always, Coe Library of the University of Wyoming was a treasure trove of useful material.

They say this is a wonderful world to live in, but I don't believe I ever did really live in a wonderful world.

—CHARLIE STARKWEATHER
in his 1958 confession

Bad Dirt

The Hellhole

O N A NOVEMBER DAY WYOMING GAME & FISH WARDEN
Creel Zmundzinski was making his way down the Pinchbutt drainage through the thickening light of late afternoon. The
last pieces of sunlight lathered his red-whiskered face with
splashes of fire. The terrain was steep with lodgepole pine giving
way on the lower slope to sagebrush and a few grassy meadows
favored by elk on their winter migration to the southeast. Occasionally, when the sight lines were clear, he caught the distant glint
of his truck and horse trailer in the gravel pullout far below. He
rode very slowly, singing of the great Joe Bob, who was ". . . the
pride of the backfield, the hero of his day";* in front of him
walked the malefactor without hunting license who had been
burying the guts of a cow moose when Creel came upon him. The
man's ATV was loaded with the hindquarters. The rest of the car-
cass had been left to rot.

"This is a protected no-hunt area," said Creel. "Let's see your
hunting license."

The ruby-complected senior slapped the many pockets in his
hunting jacket. The jacket was new, with the price tag still affixed
to the back hem. It was the flashing of the price tag that had caught

---

*Terry Allen, "The Great Joe Bob (A Regional Tragedy)," *Lubbock (on Everything)*
(Green Shoes Publishing, BMI, 1978).

Creel's eye through the trees. Now the man pulled out his wallet and foraged.

While he waited Creel Zmundzinski listened for a sound he did not want to hear.

After a long search the man handed Creel a cardboard rectangle. It was a business card, and its information contained, along with phone numbers and a greatly reduced illustration of Chartres Cathedral, the words

Reverend Jefford J. Pecker
Persia Ministry

"Where is that, Persia?" asked Creel, thinking of Iran, as the 323 area code was unfamiliar to him. He thought he heard the dreaded sound in the distance.

"Per-SEE-uh, California," said the reverend, correcting his pronunciation in a loud, nasal voice.

"That your church?" asked Creel, studying the illustration. Yes, down in the clump of willows at the base of the meadow he heard the wretched bawl of an orphan moose calf.

"It's quite similar."

"But it's sure a long way from a hunting license." His voice had become very cold. The minister did not know it, but of the fifty-three game wardens in Wyoming he had connected with the one who most hated moose cow killers who left orphan calves to figure things out for themselves in a world of predators and severe weather. For Creel Zmundzinski was an orphan himself who, after his parents were gone, lived with his aunt and uncle on their ranch in Encampment. But truancy, bad friends, and eventually, breaking and entering got him into the St. Francis Boys' Home. Smoldering with anger at the injustice of life and full of self-pity, he continued to cause trouble whenever a chance came. He might have graduated from St. Francis to the state pen in Rawlins but for Orion Horncrackle, an aging Game & Fish warden.

Warden Orion Horncrackle had enjoyed the finest kind of boy's life. He and his three older brothers had been brought up in the Buffalo Forks country of the Snake River, astride the continent, camping, riding, and hunting the Beartooth and the Buffalo Plateau wilderness in the 1930s and '40s. After World War II his surviving brothers took over the family ranch, and Orion became the first Horncrackle to attend the university in Laramie. He graduated with a degree in biology, entered the Game & Fish Department a week later, and stayed there the rest of his working life.

He was almost sixty and Creel Zmundzinski fourteen when they met. Orion was climbing the courthouse steps, and Creel, in company with two youth service officers, was lagging down, his face in a sour knot. As they drew abreast Creel kicked the warden in the ankle and smirked. The two men with him gave him a jerk that lifted him off his feet and hustled him to an old bread truck that had the words ST. FRANCIS BOYS' HOME painted on the side.

"Who's the pissed-off kid?" Orion asked the sheriff's deputy who was taking the fresh air at the top of the steps.

"One a the St. Francis bunch. They got some mean little bastards out there."

Half an hour later, his poacher a "failure to obey citation," Orion drove out into the country looking for the St. Francis Boys' Home. It was a dismal stone building standing solitary on the prairie. He could see a rough baseball diamond and a drooping basketball hoop without a net near an outbuilding with the crooked sign LAUNDRY over the door. There were no corrals, no stockyard, no barn, no garden, no mountains in view.

"What in God's name do the boys do here? Must be bored to

devilment," he told himself. He walked unchallenged around the building, got back in his truck, and left.

Back in his office he telephoned the director of the home and had a long conversation. Two Saturdays later, Orion Horncrackle, in red-shirted uniform, sat in a folding chair in a cold room in company with eleven fidgety boys, ages fourteen to seventeen, one of them Creel Zmundzinski.

"I know, boys," he said in the voice he used when talking to obstreperous horses, "that most a you think life give you a raw deal, cheated you out a parents and a home place. But you know what? That has happened to many thousands and thousands a kids and they raised theirselves up pretty good. They turned out decent. They made a mark in the world. I'm here because I want a tell you that you're not as much orphans as you think. You was born in a wonderful, wild place and I think that if you let Wyomin, your home state, and its wildlife stand in for your human parents you will do pretty good. I'm goin a help introduce you to your new folks. We will be goin up in the mountains on little trips and everbody will have to pull his weight or he won't come another trip."

"You mean like a bunch a deer will be like our mother and father?" The kid had a face like a pumpkin with incipient peach fuzz.

"Well, in a kind a way. You can learn a lot from deer."

"What about birds? I want a eagle for my dad," said Crossman, catching the idea.

"More like a skunk for *you*," said Creel, but suddenly they all began naming animals they wanted for relatives.

A very thin kid who looked half-Indian said, "Do we get to ride horses?"

"Aha! What's your name? Ramon? Right to the point. You know, it used a be you could rub a magic lamp and a genie would stick his head out a the spout and you'd say, 'Bring me couple good horses,' but them genie lamps are pretty much gone now. I'm goin a have to scratch for horses and they probably won't be the best horses in the world but I agree with you, horses are necessary, even if they are mules. And I'll get them."

He gave each of them a map of the state and talked about the Big Horns, the Sunlight Basin, the Buffalo Plateau of his own youth, the Wind River range, Towogotee Pass, Sheep Mountain, Elk Mountain, the Medicine Bow. He talked about pronghorn, mountain lion, the great elk, badgers and prairie dogs, about eagles and hawks, meadowlarks. Yellowstone Park, he said, was mostly in Wyoming and they would surely go there. He gave each of them a field guide, *Mammals of Wyoming*.

Late in the afternoon the director came tapping at the door and blurted at the boys, "Now, say thank you and goodbye to Warden Horncrackle. Time for you boys to do your compulsory exercise. Mr. Swampster is waiting in the gym. Now get cracking!"

Creel jabbed his elbow into Crossman's ribs and whispered, "He don't know he's talkin a the son a the Moose King."

"Yeah, and the son a the Gold Eagle."

"Shut up back there and get goin." To Orion Horncrackle the director said, "I doubt you can do much with this bunch. They're hardheaded."

"Troublemakers, too, I bet," said Horncrackle in his mild voice.

Creel Zmundzinski was not the only one who slept that night with his map and *Mammals of Wyoming* under his pillow, nor was he the only St. Francis kid who went on to a career in wildlife service.

"What! Hunting license! For your information, as a man of the cloth I've often received the kindly nod of local game wardens," the Reverend Jefford J. Pecker roared in his clogged-nose voice.

"That must a been in California. Sir, you are in Wyomin now and it's different. Just start down the trail in front of me. I am goin a write you a ticket for poachin." Creel Zmundzinski found it difficult to be civil to the man.

Ten minutes of outraged protest followed by a sniveling plea to be allowed to ride his ATV to the bottom as he had a medical condition did not move Creel Zmundzinski.

"What medical condition is that? You look pretty healthy to me."

"What! You're not a doctor now, are you?" screamed the man. "I have a heart condition! And a bad leg! I have nephritis!"

Creel Zmundzinski waited, and at last Reverend Pecker began walking, turning around every five minutes or so to give Creel a pithy and short sermon illustrated with many vivid phrases. Creel noticed his bad leg kept changing from left to right. It was no doubt tiring to maintain a fake limp. Every now and then Creel urged Dull Knife, his dun gelding, forward a little so that he nudged the reverend.

As they left the meadow the calf's bawling sounded loud and pathetic. Zmundzinski muttered, "Hope you make it, kid," knowing the calf didn't have a chance. When they were halfway down Creel called a sudden halt.

"Back up the trail," he said.

"What!" But the fellow walked fairly briskly up the trail, no doubt thinking they were going back for his ATV. It came to him as depressing news that the warden now insisted he carry one of the moose quarters down the trail, but still leave the ATV behind.

"What? I can't do that! That's a hundred fifty pounds of fucking meat!"

"I'll help you load up, Reverend Pottymouth," said the warden kindly.

"Pecker!" shrieked the furious preacher. "My name is *Pecker*!"

"You bet," said Creel.

The Hellhole

It took a long time to get to the bottom of the trail as the hunter kept sagging against trees and claiming he had to rest.

"All right, now back up for the other one."

"*What!* You're going to pay for this, you rotten red shirt asshole. I know some *people*. I'll see your head on a platter. I'll have you *fired* and I'll have your *boss* fired and I'll make sure he knows *why* he was canned. Because of *you*."

In the gravel pullout Creel allowed the man to drop the second load of meat in the back of the state truck. Dirty and blood-stained, the preacher stood on a slightly depressed patch of gravel near the far end of the pullout. As soon as he caught his breath he began listing the reasons Creel should not write him a citation. Those reasons included the painful pangs of conscience that would certainly cause Creel grief later, the lawsuit the reverend intended to file against Wyoming Game & Fish, and the reverend's powerful friends who would make life a constant misery for a certain redheaded warden whose ancestors were undoubtedly related to Torquemada, Bill Clinton, and the Pope. Creel continued to write.

"You fucking hear me? You shithead warden, you're going to burn in *Hell*!" shouted the excited man, and he stamped his feet and jumped in frustration and rage. Tendrils of smoke rose in a circle around him.

"What?" he said as the gravel sagged beneath his feet. There was a sound like someone tearing a head of lettuce apart. The gravel heaved and abruptly gaped open. The hunter dropped down into a fiery red tube about three feet across that resembled an enormous blowtorch-heated pipe. With a shriek the preacher disappeared. The whole thing had happened in less than five seconds.

Immediately the entrance to the hot conduit closed up and the gravel of the turnaround looked undisturbed and solid except for a slightly soot-darkened circular depression marking the fatal entrance. There was a faint sulfurous odor, not unlike that of the tap water in Zmundzinski's trailer kitchen back in Elk Tooth. The horse shivered but stood his ground.

"My God," said Creel to Dull Knife. "Did that happen? Did we see that?" He walked gingerly toward the circular depression. He thought he could hear a distant and faint sizzling sound. He bent over and held his hand just above the gravel where the Reverend Pecker had stood only minutes before. It was definitely warm. He found a twenty-pound rock and dropped it on the spot. The gravel seemed to stir a little, but no fiery hole opened up. After half an hour of puzzled examination and deep thought he gave up and drove home in the dark. He didn't know what had happened, but it had saved a lot of paperwork.

A week later Creel Zmundzinski had a rancorous run-in with two Texas lawyers and their friend, a California IRS agent, who swore Creel would be audited every year of his future life, and that his children and his children's children would also be audited.

"Another good reason not to git married," said Creel.

The lawyers said he would do hard time in a maximum-security cell.

"I sure hope it won't be in the cell next a yours," he said, smiling.

None of them had Wyoming hunting licenses, although two produced Texas licenses and claimed there was a reciprocal agreement between Texas and Wyoming to honor each other's licenses. Creel laughed and said he didn't think so. The men had cut off the heads of the five bull elk they had shot, abandoning the carcasses in an irrigation ditch, clogging it and causing it to overflow. He made them clean out the ditch, dig a pit, and bury the flyblown carcasses, then drive ahead of him to the Pinchbutt pullout.

He was careful to park near the road. It was a pullout to be approached with caution. He prodded them toward the far end.

"Just stand over there," he directed, pointing to where the gravel had a darker color.

They slouched carelessly in the direction he was pointing. The faint circular depression was almost invisible, but he recognized it by the rock he had dropped after the Reverend Pecker's quick exit and the darker gravel that marked the perimeter of the opening. He supposed it was soot that discolored the edges. He took up his citation book wondering how to get them to jump up and down or stamp. He didn't even know if that would work. Maybe Preacher Pecker had been an isolated case. Maybe it only worked with backsliding ministers. Maybe some kind of cosmic forces had been in alignment. He pretended to ponder, putting his pen to his lips and tilting his head to one side.

"Gentlemen, tell you what. I'll let you go this time if you'll take part in a silly little thing. For my own personal satisfaction, if I'm goin a let you go I want a see you look ridiculous first. I'd like you to give a little jump—like this"—and he demonstrated—"and then I'll laugh, but I won't write you up."

The three friends looked at one another and made faces indicating they were dealing with a lunatic.

"Let's humor the man," said the IRS agent, and he gave a tiny jump, barely an inch. Nothing happened, but Creel saw a single faint tendril of smoke in the right place.

"Come on, make it a good jump," he said, leaping high himself to encourage them.

One of the lawyers sprang into the air with a grace that Creel admired, and as the man landed, the ground opened beneath the trio and they dropped into the glowing borehole. The IRS man had been standing with one foot outside the circle, and for a moment it seemed he might escape, but the tunnel exerted a powerful suction. Creel could feel it from twenty feet away as he watched the IRS man whisk in like a fly into a vacuum cleaner nozzle.

So, he thought, the trick was in getting them to jump. It was a wonderful discovery, and he wasted no time in telling his fellow wardens the secret of the Pinchbutt pullout. The Hellhole, as he called it, saved a great deal of tedious paperwork and became so popular that sometimes several Game & Fish trucks were lined up along the road waiting a turn at the facilities. Wardens drove many miles to get outlaws to the wonderful hole. One wrongdoer, after a three-hour drive, threatened to sue for cruel and inhuman detention as the interior of the warden's truck reeked of wet dog, manure, offal, and sardine sandwiches. There is no record that such a suit was ever filed.

They were all sworn to secrecy. Creel did not even tell his closest friend, Plato Bucklew.

The next season Creel Zmundzinski clumped into his favorite bar, Pee Wee's in Elk Tooth. He sat at a back table where Plato Bucklew sat drinking boilermakers and reading the lonely hearts columns in the paper. Creel sighed, ostentatiously. Plato looked up.

"Matter with you? Didn't get any bad guys today?"

"Got plenty. My hand's about wore out from writin tickets. Gimme the same thing," he said to Amanda Gribb, waving his hand at Plato's beverages.

"So your hand is wore out—nothin unusual in that, is there?" He put a salacious twist on the question.

"It's goin a be like that the rest a the season, thanks to the goddamn Forest Circus."

"What's that supposed a mean?"

"It means the goddamn Forest Circus screwed up the best deal I ever had." And he told him the complete story about the

Hellhole, about the line of wardens waiting to use it, about the unearthly shrieks of malefactors as they slid down into the brimstone.

"And? What's Forest got a do with it?" Plato Bucklew worked for the Forest Service, and as much as he complained about his hardheaded, shortsighted bosses he did not like to hear a redshirt, even Creel, put the organization down.

"Tell you what, I got me a bad nasty one today, cocky little rat works in a bakery in Iron Mule, killed a doe. Then he drops his pants and gets down on the ground and proceeds to have sexual relations with the dead doe. And I'm standin about twenty feet away."

"Jesus!" Plato inhaled his whiskey the wrong way. "That's"—he drew on his course in criminal psychology—"that's like deviant bestial necrophilia! What'd you write him up for?"

"Nothin, except he was in a buck-only area. Game laws don't say a word about deviant hunter necrofoliage or whatever."

"Well, look at the bright side. It could a been a lot more writin. At least it wasn't a buck—then it would a been homosexual deviant bestial necrophilia. So what did you do?"

"So I tell him to get his pants up and I take him to that certain pulloff and things sure look different. Looks like the Forest Service had a convention a road scrapers and backhoes in there. It's all opened up, room for fifty cars, fancy trailhead signs, posts, two a the new shitters, garbage can, trail maps, the works. But I can't figure out where the sweet spot was. I walked all over that place, smackin the ground with a fence post Forest left layin on the bank, and nothin. Nothin! I got the guy standin there watchin me. He must a thought I was nuts. In the end I had a write him a regular ticket. I told the other wardens, and at lunch we was all there, jumpin around, pokin at the gravel, tryin a find that sweet, sweet spot. Total *nada*. It's gone."

"Kind a hard a believe it was ever there. You didn't say nothin about it last year. Sounds like hyperactive imagination. Or mass hypnosis."

"I wish you'd never took that damn criminal psychology course. It was a *secret*. Couldn't tell anybody."

"Suppose so? There was a memo come in late last fall to Jumbo Nottage about a lot a traffic out there at that pulloff. Parkin problem. I guess he thought maybe it was a good place for multiple use enlargement. He probly thought the traffic was tourists and day-trippers. Didn't occur to him that Game & Fish was roastin citizens in there like ears a corn." He signaled Amanda Gribb.

"Amanda? Ain't there a mix drink called the Devil's Somethin-or-Other?"

"I'll look in the book." Amanda had been trying to hear the low-voiced conversation but missed everything except "bestial necrophilia," which Plato had pronounced in a rather loud voice.

"Yep, there's somethin called a Devil's Tail. It's made with vodka, rum, and apricot brandy."

"That's it. Give us two a those. Doubles. In honor a my friend, Warden Creel, who pulled the devil's tail all last year and wants a do it again."

The Indian Wars Refought

ONE SUMMER DAY AROUND THE TURN OF THE LAST century, two men in overalls, one holding a roofing hammer, stood in a Casper street and looked at a new building.

"I guess that'll show the cow crowd who's got the big sugar in this town," said one.

The other man smiled as though testing his lips and said, "One or two, maybe. You should a went into lawyerin, Verge, it'd be *your* buildin we are puttin up."

"Rather have a ranch. That's where the real money lays."

"There he is right now," said the man with the hammer, nodding at the tall frock-coated figure striding toward them with his scissory gait. He did not look at them but at the building.

"Well, well, boys," said lawyer Gay G. Brawls. "That's the queen of Casper, and we're the ones put her up."

In the decades after statehood every Wyoming town had to have at least one imposing building. These banks, courthouses, opera halls, hotels, railroad stations, and commercial buildings were constructed of local-quarry stone, of concrete blocks shaped to resemble stone, and some were iron-fronts ordered from catalogs. Few have held on to their original purpose and so today a cell phone company operates incongruously in a handsome opera house, and the ornate Sweetwater Brewery is occupied by a fence company.

The iron-front Brawls Commercial gave the impression of a kind of extravagant prosperity, surrounded as it was by flimsy false-front wood structures. The various parts of the building—a handsome cornice, pilasters that separated windows and doors, a lintel stamped with Egyptian motifs separating the ground floor from the upper story—had all been shipped by railroad from St. Louis. A neoclassical entry with garlanded cornices and inset colored glass distinguished the front. On that summer day in 1900 lawyer Gay G. Brawls carried his own papers to his new office upstairs. The ground floor housed a dry-goods shop behind the town's first plate-glass window and featured bolts of calico, fustian, and trimmings. In the back was an up-to-date selection of men's suits, which the proprietor, Mr. Isaac Frasket, altered to fit the broad-shouldered, small-waisted cowboys who plunged for the outfits. He paid an extra rent to store hatboxes and millinery supplies in one of the rooms on the second floor, side by side with boxes of old depositions, wills, and case notes.

Brawls' practice was busy and select. The best-known of his clients was William F. Cody—Buffalo Bill. Lawyer Brawls, in concert with other legal beagles, helped the showman teeter along the edges of his various bankruptcies occasioned by business dealings with the infamous Denver newspaper and circus entrepreneurs, Bonfils and Tammen.

Lawyer Brawls, thirty-three years old when his building went up, had long horseman's legs, black hair as fine as cat fur, and a beard shadow like a mask. He was almost a handsome man, his appearance spoiled only by a reddish mole on his left eyelid, but the brilliant aquamarine color of his irises pulled attention away from that flaw. He seemed made for the saddle but suffered an allergy to horses at a time when horses were transportation. Even ten minutes in an open carriage set his eyes streaming and a clenching headache ricocheting behind his eyes, so he walked everywhere, and if a destination was too far to travel by shank's mare he didn't go. He owned one of the first motorcars in Casper.

In 1919 Mr. Frasket, the old dry-goods merchant, died and his corpse was shipped back east. An ice cream parlor rented the premises and became a popular gathering place. Seven months later Gay G. Brawls himself, on his way back up to his office after a lemon phosphate, dropped some business folders on the stairs, stumbled and slipped on them, cracked his head, and after a week in a coma, died at age fifty-three.

His son, Archibald Brawls, also a lawyer, and as tall and dark as his father and with the same blue eyes and born-to-the-saddle cowboy good looks except for a mouthful of bad teeth, moved into the second-floor offices. His hours in the dentist's chair taught him something of pain.

"Mr. Brawls," said the dentist, "I can make you a good set a nut-crackers, pull out these diseased teeth, and after she heals up, with the new plates you'll be free from pain forever. And the new set will look good, not like these bad gappy ones."

"Do it," said Brawls, and within a month his bad old ivories had been replaced with dentures that seemed carved from a glacier.

Archibald Brawls' business was lively in the 1920s, despite his youth. He acted for an important rancher north of Casper, a man with political connections whose deeded land abutted the Emergency Naval Oil Reserve No. 3, just then becoming infamous as Teapot Dome. The rancher, John Bucklin, had more than once dined with the Interior Secretary, Albert B. Fall, a political animal who wrested control of the reserve away from the Navy and then leased it to oilman Harry Sinclair in a classic sweetheart deal. Fall was a man who disdained the nascent conservation movement in favor of full-throttle resource exploitation, setting a certain tone for the future. Big money changed hands and Bucklin worried about being swept into the government's dustpan of investigation. The accumulating legal paper crowded Brawls' office. But, as he said, showing his icy smile, it's an ill wind that doesn't blow somebody a little good. The Teapot scandal was a turning point in his career, and after Fall went to prison, young lawyer Brawls' interests shifted from petty affairs such as deeds and wills to representation of timber and oil interests, railroads, irrigation rights settlement, and the wonderfully cloudy law of mineral leases.

He increased his storage space, stacking his father's papers and books in the back of a deep closet. He added his own legal junk, the boxes jammed high and tight.

He made money all through the Depression. Others in Natrona County got rich as well. While the rest of the country was suffering dust storms and bread lines, Casper enjoyed a flood of oil profits. It set off a building boom. The Brawls Commercial was no longer the premier structure in the town.

In 1939 Archibald Brawls bought a ranch north of Casper—the former property of Bucklin, whom he had counseled in the Teapot Dome affair—and on weekends began to live the life of a distinguished rancher. It pleased him to improve his herd with pedigreed stock. The property was mostly yardang and trough, the tops of the ridges shaved smooth by eons of westerlies. It lay just on the northern edge of the great wind corridor that sweeps the state from the Red Desert to the Nebraska border. But, although Brawls and his wife, Kate, a blond with a face she had clipped from a magazine and the caramel eyes of a lizard, entertained important politicians and ranchers, although their New Year's galas and Fourth of July ranch barbecues were great events in Wyoming society, somehow their lives were tragic. Brawls wanted to build up a ranch kingdom with his boys, but his oldest son, Vivian, was killed in the Second World War. Basford, the second son, who was something of a drinker, steered his Ford into a fatal draw and died alone in the sagebrush. Then Kate sued for divorce, moved to

Denver, and remarried a podiatrist. The third son, Sage, graduated from Boston University Law School in 1959 and joined his father's practice. He always wore a suit, in contrast to his father's boots, twill pants, and many-pocketed vest.

"Somebody in this outfit has to look like a lawyer," he joked.

Archibald raised one eyebrow, exposed his cold teeth. "You still don't know, even at your age, that it's ranching interests run this state? They come to us because they recognize"—and here he hooked a thumb in his vest armhole, omnipresent cigarette dribbling ash down the front—"that we *know* their problems." He adjusted his Stetson, which like a Texas sheriff, he always wore in the office.

Clients saw how strongly the Brawls men resembled one another, compared the framed photograph of Gay G. Brawls that hung in the anteroom with the living examples of Archibald and Sage. They were all rangy, all with heavy dark beards that showed immediately after they shaved, all too tall for doorways. When finally Archibald Brawls died of lung cancer in 1962, the year lightning demolished the stubby spout of Teapot Dome, his Sinclair stock and his holdings in the oil-rich Salt Creek fields north of Casper had made him wealthy. The son, Sage, inherited the ranch, the law practice, the money.

Sage Brawls, after a notorious period of wild-oats sowing, married Georgina Crawshaw of Wheatland, fifteen years younger than he. Her great-grandfather, Waile Crawshaw, had been known throughout the west as a sharp judge of horseflesh. In 1910 he had bought dozens of fine thoroughbreds for the proverbial song in New York when that state moved against horse racing and the thoroughbred market crashed. He shipped them to Wyoming and bred them to his polo ponies. His children continued the business, and Crawshaw mounts played on the polo fields of the world.

Georgina, raised on the family ranch, was as blond as Sage's mother, but thin and athletic, with a body like that of a strong boy.

She had big, wiry hands and bit her thumbnails. It was she who introduced Sage to polo and crossword puzzles.

They had no children, and perhaps this accounted for the ossification of Sage's interests and character. As a child he had had an inquiring mind, had caught snowflakes on a piece of black velvet, wondered how many lodgepole pollen grains were in the yellow mountain clouds of summer, worked mathematical puzzles. But Georgina won him over to polo, and within a few years he thought of little else. The crosswords were too much for him.

Like many who admire horses, Sage Brawls let his affection become an obsession. He loved the sport, the gallop, the danger, the players' athletic skills, the aggressive thrust of the riding-off maneuver, the heavy breathing, the smell of dust and torn grass, even the sight of the spectators, heads bent like those of treasure seekers after coins, replacing divots of turf between chukkas. Polo in Wyoming was not exclusively the sport of the wealthy but also the pleasure of ranch hands and working people. Individual riding skill counted for more than money, but as Sage sometimes remarked, it didn't hurt if you had both. He was handicapped at 6 and Georgina, who was a ferociously expert horsewoman, at 7.

Sage's clients became inured to the sight of their lawyer suddenly twisting around until he touched the ground behind his left heel with his right hand. When he rose in the morning he did other flexibility exercises that a later generation would have recognized as yoga. The Brawls had a polo pit built where they could practice difficult strokes. There were photographs throughout their house—Sage delivering a nearside forehand shot, an offside under-the-neck stroke, posing sweaty and triumphant with his team, and one of Georgina mounted on Quickstep, holding the Wyoming Cup.

The years rolled along, and little by little Sage neglected his law practice as it kept him from polo matches. Time and money went into their ponies, and they built a second house in Sheridan

so they could be nearer the Big Horn Polo Club. On a seniors'
match trip to Omaha on the last day of June in 1994, when Sage
was riding Cold Air, a new mount he was trying out, a spectator's
child, impatient for the Fourth of July, set off a forbidden bottle
rocket that struck the animal on the flank. Now in his early sixties,
Sage Brawls was no longer lithe and flexible. Arthritis had seized
his hips and shoulders despite his exercises. A few years earlier he
would have been able to spring free. The terrified animal reared
and fell over backward, crushing the rider. Two days later he
died, and that was that. The Brawls, as the dinosaurs, were gone
from Wyoming.

Georgina, grieving and guilt-ridden, sold most of the ponies,
donated Sage's and her own tack and mallets to the polo club, and
swore to leave the sport. Decker Mell, who played the number
one position on her team, telephoned, Decker with his face like an
arrowhead, eyes so pale a blue they looked turned inside out, and
atop his lip a drizzly mustache. He was a brand inspector with a
weakness for horseflesh.

"I had real mixed feelins when I heard you give your gear to the
Club. Goddamn, Georgina, don't do this, throw everthing away.
Your friends, your family, your life is mixed right up with polo."

"The sport didn't do me any favors." She could imagine him
spitting into the telephone, the black pupils of those faded eyes
like exclamation points.

"Georgina, think a the history. It's more than the team and the
matches, it's more than playing, and you are a wonderful athlete."

"Startin a feel my age, Deck. Sage wouldn't quit, even when he
stiffened up. You see what it got him?"

"O.K., I can understand that, but remember that your people
been connected for generations to polo—they knew the Mon-
creiffs, the Wallops, and wasn't your great-granddaddy related by

marriage to the Gallatins? I mean, there's *history* there. You got a responsibility."

"Yeah, but—"

"Crawshaw is one a the great names in western polo. I personally won't let you get out. We need you, we need a keep the Crawshaw name alive in polo."

They met for lunch, and Georgina said that while she would not play again, she could become an involved spectator, a keeper of records and local polo history. The connections would live on.

"You could be an umpire, Georgina."

"You think so? I cannot see that happening," she said. "There are no women umpires that I ever heard of."

"First time for everthing," he said. "Or you could be the timekeeper." That was more like it. She could be a timekeeper.

Then, suddenly, she remarried, her surprise choice the ranch foreman, Charlie Parrott, considerably younger than she and part Oglala Sioux, or so he claimed, though she figured Mexican and something else was in there but what of it? Parrott, with a tight, hard body and buttocks like cantaloupes, had a long swatch of black hair, glittering black eyes behind wire-rimmed glasses. His sad, big face and frog-wide mouth did not go with his body, but the low voice pulled things together. He had hired on only weeks before Sage's death. Charlie was not a great fan of polo, but horses liked him for his quiet, slow movements, his silence, his affection, felt more than observed. Georgina liked him for some of the same reasons. If Sage had known of his lack of interest in polo he would have told the man to move on. But Georgina didn't care.

"Anyhow, I don't have to play polo to manage a horse ranch," said Charlie Parrott. "That's what you got Elwyn for." Elwyn Gaines, middle-aged and spattered with transparent freckles, was the soft-spoken trainer and married to the Brawlses' cook, Doreen Gaines. Their son, Press, worked as a groom, cleaning tack and mucking out stalls. Georgina said she would rather have her head shaved than lose any of the Gaineses.

Georgina found Charlie Parrott more than attractive. There had not been much sex with Sage in the last years, but once Charlie got going he was insatiable and she found herself heated to the point of abandoned vulgarity.

"Look at this," she would say and haul up her nightgown.

"Take that damn thing off." And he was on her like a falling I-beam.

He had been married twice before, the first time to a woman who now lived in Nevada and with her had had one daughter, Linny. The second wife, he said, was a California cop, and they broke up after five months of screaming. End of story. In his slow, easy voice he gave his daughter Linny's history; she was in her early twenties and apparently a pure Nevada hellcat who had already been the recipient of two unwanted pregnancies. Linny was coming to live with them, Charlie Parrott told his widow-bride. A flash of distaste crossed her features. She covered up quickly with a grand smile.

"Well, it'll be nice to have another woman on the place," she said, but with some acid, as if remarking that it would be nice to have more rattlesnakes. Charlie Parrott wasn't fooled and told Linny to walk softly. The girl's name had been picked from a baby-name book which reflected a brief fashion of naming girls for expensive wedding gifts of an earlier time—Linen, Silver, Crystal, Ivory.

When Georgina told Decker Mell, who had become her confidant, of this new development he remarked that she was probably in for some trouble.

"You know, Georgina, I sort a wish you hadn't married him. You should a hitched up with somebody in polo. I am guessin Charlie don't have much feelin for polo."

"Right," she laughed, implying that her husband had an excellent feel for other, unspecified sports. "But you were already married, Decker, so I had to settle for Charlie." They both laughed.

Linny arrived on an August weekend driving an old Land Rover with a bad muffler, the vehicle once painted with tiger stripes now faded to faint wiggles. She was wearing a skimpy green halter and the shortest skirt Georgina had ever seen. She was a big, good-looking girl, buxom and curvaceous, with dusty black hair (except for a fringe of bleached blond bangs) pulled into a ponytail that slapped her between the shoulder blades when she ran. She looked very Indian to Georgina, more Indian than Charlie. Her face contained enough material for two faces: a high brow, a long chin, wide cheekbones with fleshy cheeks like vehicle headrests, and a nose like a plowshare. Her eyes were black, double-size almonds, and her long teeth were perfect. Georgina saw that Linny's eyes were marred by a slight strabismus in the left one which gave her a crazy appearance as though she might suddenly shriek and spring on someone. She yanked two huge duffel bags out of the Land Rover.

Georgina and Linny shook hands like men, eyeing each other as though looking for toeholds.

Linny said, "I sure appreciate it that you let me come here. It's my plan to find a job and then get an apartment or something in town. I don't want to get in your and Dad's way." She scratched her dark thigh with mint green nails.

"That sounds like a plan, Linny. I'm happy to help if I can. The job thing might be tough. Wyoming is not a great place for jobs. What kind a work have you been doin?"

"Mostly I been in school, little bit a film school in California, which I couldn't hack after they showed us this nasty old Edison film, *Electrocution of an Elephant*. Then I worked in Reno at one of the casinos."

"The elephant thing does sound ugly. But Reno?"

"Sure. My mother lives in Reno. She works in one a the casinos and I got a job in the gift shop. You know, waitin on customers. Somebody wins some money, first thing they want a do is spend it. And the gift shop had real expensive stuff. It was sort of a crappy job, though. But paid pretty good so the employees wouldn't try to rip the shop off. That's how I could afford the Land Rover. And I did other stuff. The usual, like, let's see, I did waitressing, bartending, and the gift shop thing, then a summer as a fire spotter in this lookout tower for the Forest Service. Which was a headache—those horny USFS guys would come up there all the time to 'help me out.'"

"Uh-huh," said Georgina, biting back a remark that anyone who wore clothes as skimpy as Linny's would always be bothered by men with horn colic, and went off to the kitchen to talk with the cook.

Doreen Gaines was a thin hypochondriac. She and her husband had worked for the Brawlses since 1978. After Sage's death she stayed on, the main artery of news connecting the Brawlses to the town. Sage and Georgina had given the Gaineses an unvarying Christmas present—a hundred-dollar bill and a saddle blanket. They had twenty-four saddle blankets, most with the price stickers still on them, stacked on top of the freezer in their garage. While Sage Brawls was alive Doreen had recognized Georgina as the enemy, but now Charlie Parrott and his half-naked daughter had moved into the opponent's corner.

"Dad," said Linny to Charlie Parrott, "she's too old to have kids, right?"

"Who, Georgina? I guess so. Never discussed it. Guess she's

over the line. Never thought about more kids, seeing how bad the first one turned out." He winked at her, but there rose in his mind like a bubble elevating through beer the image of his first wife, whom he had not seen for years, her little razory face and dark-circled eyes. In his memory it was a very cold day so that he, coming out of a humid and overheated house, had taken in breaths of air that seemed slabs of clear, thin ice. The sunlight all around her flashed with snow crystals that emerged from the empty air rather than falling from clouds, for the sky was blue.

"I mean, she's older than you—like, she must be fifty—well, like it's a pretty nice ranch. Too bad it's so far out from town." And the girl squinted at the horizon. Her father was a good-looking man who had played the sexual attraction card well. She understood the game.

Charlie Parrott caught the drift of these remarks; Linny was figuring the odds on someday inheriting the Brawlses' ranch but didn't want to come right out and say it. He'd done the same figuring himself. They were a pair.

"What's your mother do these days?"

"Workin. She got a chambermaid job at one a the casinos. The Big Lucky Palace."

"She still hit the bottle?"

"What a *you* think? Why I'm here."

After the dinner dishes were cleared Linny would fire up her old Land Rover and take off for Casper. She would drag in long after midnight, and sometimes, when it was very late, park down near the main road and walk in to the ranch house. The dogs never barked at her. At breakfast she always said she'd been job hunting, that the best place to find out about jobs was not in the newspapers but in the bars.

"You know," said Georgina to Charlie in the night, "this trottin off to the bars every night is goin a end in number three."

"Number three what?"

"Number three knocked up," said Georgina. "You pay for the other abortions?"

"Yeah. You know, I'm her father and all. She counts on me."

"I can see that."

"All she needs is a job. She gets a job she'll straighten out pretty fast. She's a good girl."

Georgina thought Linny was more of a ripe young slut, but she said nothing.

"Hey," said Charlie Parrott. "Come on over here." And he reached for her, his callused hands catching on the silk of her nightgown.

Georgina experienced a quick memory of the aging Sage Brawls trying to twist down and put his right hand on the floor behind his left heel.

A few days later Georgina cornered Linny at noon. The girl, wearing nothing but a T-shirt and sagging, blood-spotted briefs, was at the counter, fixing her breakfast, a plate of tortillas and beans with huge amounts of fiery salsa. Fighting a hangover, Georgina suspected. Doreen was kneading bread, shooting glances at Linny. Georgina waved her out into the garden, then, as Linny sat at the table, Georgina swung her bony behind onto a stool near the counter. Her rough heels scraped the rungs.

"Got a proposition for you. There's this buildin down in Casper belonged to Mr. Brawls—the Brawls Commercial. They owned it for years and years. Now I get this notice that the city wants a condemn it, tear it down. They'll pay somethin for it, but that's not the point—they want it gone. Casper's upgradin. So, we got a few weeks, a month, clean out the buildin. I went down there yesterday and took a look. The structure's in bad shape. And there's file cabinets full a papers, boxes a papers, rooms a boxes. Some a this paper might be important. The Brawlses had their hand in a lot a things. I talked to some a the State Archives people. They would like to know what's there. They'll probly take most of it off our hands. But I don't just want a turn it over without knowin what we got. So, I need for somebody go through those boxes. Keep a eye out for letters from George Warshinton or whatever. See what turns up, make some kind a list. You want the job?"

"How's the pay?"

She named a good figure, enough money for Linny to pack her suitcases and head for California or Phoenix and lead her own life when the job was done.

"Works for me," said the girl, sticking out her hot, dry hand.

"We'll go down this afternoon, look it over, make you a key. And you might want a change your underwear."

"O.K. if I came in now?" said Doreen at the door in an aggrieved voice. "I got to get that bread goin."

The Brawls Commercial building stood slumped and weary, its foundation breached. The interior stank. Even though it was downtown it smelled as if several skunks had got under the floor and died. The plaster, wet and dried for years from a growing leak in the roof, added its own tongue-curling flavor. Dust, peeling wallpaper, dry rot, and rodent tenants gave off an effluvium that made Linny retch.

"It's worse than it was yesterday," Georgina said. "If that's possible. We'll get some windows open. Bring some room freshener in. The electricity don't work so a fan don't work neither."

Upstairs Linny heaved at the windows, finally got a cross-draft whose hot, dry air began sucking the stink away. Sage Brawls' desk was still littered with his brittle papers. The dust that lay on the arms and back of his chair like fur strips shuddered in the fresh breeze.

"God knows what the clients did. He didn't have so many there at the end, I guess."

Linny went into the next room, pulling open wooden filing cabinet drawers that stuck and squalled like wildcats when forced. She opened a closet and saw boxes of more papers. None of the boxes were labeled beyond small Roman numerals in the lower left hand corners.

"They are sort of numbered," said Linny. "How much is IIC? I hate those old Roman numerals. How did they ever multiply or divide?"

"Who knows?" said Georgina, who had dropped out of school early and to whom "Latin" meant Tito Puente and margaritas.

Georgina wanted to stay and watch Linny, tell her what to do, but throttled the urge to control.

"O.K.," she said. "I'll leave you to it."

Late that afternoon the old Land Rover rolled in. Charlie Parrott was just closing the tack room door and looked over at his daughter.

"What the hell you been doin?" he said. "Christ, look at you." The girl was streaked with sweat-runneled dirt and dust. Her damp hair straggled. There were cuts on her arms, and she sneezed.

"Dust." She wept. "Cleanin up the old Brawls files for Georgina. That fuckin buildin's got more dust and rat turds in it and dead moths and mice glued onto the floor than Nevada's got sand."

"She payin you?"

"You bet. Good pay, but a stinkin job."

"She didn't say nothing a *me* about it." He moved his jaw from side to side, pushed up on his glasses. "What's them cuts on your arms? Look like hunderd and elevens."

"From those old file folders. They're all dried out and sharp on the edges. What's hundred and elevens?"

"Old-timers used a call the spur marks on a hard-rode horse 'hunderd and elevens.'" He drew the marks /// in the dust to illustrate. "Well, hell, why not bring the vacuum cleaner down there and get rid a that dirt? If you're goin a do this? Simple enough."

"No electricity. Buildin's dead. They're gettin ready a tear it down. Pretty soon."

"Baby girl, they invented a thing called a generator. Tomorrow mornin I'll come down and set up a genny for you. Get that dust out anyway. We'll take the Shop-Vac, not upset the household arrangements. What all is down there anyhow?"

"Dad, those old Brawlses never threw a thing away. It is letters of all kinds to about ever person in the world, court stuff, law books. Hard a know where to begin. Mr. Gay Brawls. What a name!"

"It didn't use to mean what it means now. Plenty were named Gay. Even in Nevada. Was old Gay Pitch had a gas station in Winnemucca. Nobody thought nothin about it and he raised a railroad car a kids. So, O.K., tomorrow morning I'll drop in."

Whatever it was, they were in it together.

The next day they spent the forenoon vacuuming and cleaning. Charlie Parrott lugged several pails of water up the stairs and sloshed them over the floor to lay the dust. It was another day before Linny got at the closet where Gay G. Brawls' working life was stored.

*　　*　　*

Georgina had seen Charlie loading the generator into the truck and, when he said he had to go to town, immediately guessed its purpose. She telephoned Decker Mell.

"He's takin the generator down to town. Bet you he is goin a clean up all the dust in that building for her. She come home yesterday some mess a dirt."

"That seems kind a sensible," said Decker. "What's the problem?"

"Oh, no problem yet, but he didn't *say* nothin about it to me. You'd think he'd a mentioned it. He babies that girl too much."

But that night at dinner Charlie remarked in his offhand way that he had cleaned up the dust for Linny and that she was ripping through the old papers with a sense of determination that amazed him.

"She's a good kid," he said, and the parent and daughter smiled at each other.

"You ought a told me she was doin this job," he said in an offhand way to Georgina, who did not reply but cut savagely at the meat on her plate.

Linny opened another of Gay G. Brawls' boxes. Inside she found a sheaf of letters, many from someone who signed himself "Bill," and at the bottom of the box, half a dozen cans of film marked with Roman numerals. What, she wondered, was the appeal of Roman numerals to those old dead lawyers? She read several letters, one dated October 1913 from "Wounded Knee Battlefield." The writer, whose name she could not make out, had a spiky black hand, and addressed lawyer Brawls as "Gay."

We left Chicago 13 days ago and are here to reproduce the battle of Wounded Knee for the moving picture machine. It is Col. Cody's big project and he has high hopes that it will relieve him of debt. I am a little concerned about this as Messers. Bonfils and Tammen are backing the affair which will be filmed and produced by Essanay—the Chicago film company—and the Colonel seems only to fall behind in these partnerships. We must hope for the best. He will do other battles—Summit Springs, the Mission, last stand of the Cheyennes, etc. We are surrounded by Indians and their teepees and the soldiers of the 7th Cav. from Fort Robinson. The Indians are always here with an interpreter powwowing about the rations they are to get or the acting pay or something or other. It's been really cold.

Another letter, in the same handwriting:

General Miles, who is the advisor, is very fussy about accuracy, insisted that as there were 11,000 U.S. troops under his command back then, that many must be shown. It was amusing that while Col. Cody agreed to this, the same 300 troops marched around and around until 11,000 were shown! The moving picture machine had no film in it!

There was a yellowed newspaper clipping, so dry and weak the edges crumbled when she touched it. She laid it on a chair and read the remaining portions of a rave review headlined: "Great Audience Held in Tense Wonder by Indian War Pictures."

The reviewer wrote that the pictures were "very wonderful in their realism. It is quite impossible to describe them. They are something we can never see again." On and on the review went, conjuring flying snow, the barking of the machine guns, dying Indians, drifting smoke. Finally, wrote the deeply moved reporter,

... we were recalled to the fact that we were sitting in the Tabor Opera house looking at the moving picture reproduction of the last fight of the Indians of North America against the army of the

United States. Hillsides, the plains, the moving troops, the dying Indians, the coughing Hotchkiss were no more. Instead there were the lights of the theatre and the white screen and a thousand people awaking to the realization of having witnessed the most wonderful spectacle ever produced since moving pictures were invented. . . . Nothing like this has ever been done before. Nothing to equal it will perhaps, ever be done again.

Linny sighed and carefully laid the fragile paper in a folder. She picked up one of the film canisters. "War Bonnet #II," read the faded label. Roman numerals again. "Rebellion/Reel No. I" was another. There were five Rebellion canisters. But what rebellion? She had only a hazy idea of the Indian wars. Perhaps she would go to the library. She knew better than to open any film canisters.

That evening, watching the news, when Georgina left the room to go to the bathroom, she said to Charlie Parrott, "I found somethin today *might* be interestin."

"What?"

"Cans a film. Letters from Buffalo Bill. Seems like he was makin a movie of the Indians and the U.S. Army fights. I guess maybe that's the film in those cans."

"Yeah? First I heard about a movie like that."

"It was way back in 1913 he made it. I got a check it out at the library, see what I can find out. Might be valuable."

"The letters probly worth somethin. What'd they say?" He turned the television sound off.

"Just legal stuff, stuff about debts and payments and some letters about the film, about them being in some place called Wounded Knee. Weird name. In South Dakota?"

Charlie Parrott snapped his head up. "Wounded Knee! My God, did that old fraud have anything to do with Wounded Knee?"

"I guess so. What about it? What was Wounded Knee, anyway?"

But Georgina came into the room and made a face at their conversation, turned the television sound back on.

"I'll tell you tomorrow. It's a long story."

"What's a long story?" asked Georgina.

"Indian history," said Charlie Parrott. "A long, sad story that makes you want a puke."

Charlie spent the next day sorting out the neighboring ranch's cattle that had found a weak section of fence and breached it. When he got back at dusk, dirty and tired, Linny and Georgina had eaten and cleared the table. There was a place for him set in the kitchen.

"Georgina said keep your supper warm," said Doreen. "But it ain't the kind a supper that keeps good. Kind a dried out," she said, taking a plate of steak and baked potato out of the oven. The potato had the feel of a deflated football, though smaller. The steak had curled up on the edges and showed the reticulate grain of an osprey's leg.

Doreen talked on. "And Georgina went up to some polo meetin in Sheridan. Said she might stay over. Said she would call you around ten." He nodded. He preferred she stay over than drive at night, when all the raging drunks were on the highway looking for something to hit.

"Anyway," said Doreen, "I'm out a here."

Linny came in, dressed in her bar clothes—short skirt, peewee boots, and a tiny halter.

"I was goin a tell you about Indian stuff?" he said. It was the ideal time with Georgina out and the long evening stretching ahead.

"Don't bother," she said. "I went to the library and got a stack a books." She gestured at the counter where several books lay. He could see the library call numbers. "I'm just goin downtown for a hour. I'll start readin when I get back."

After she left he looked at the books. The top one was Dee Brown's *Bury My Heart at Wounded Knee*. "She won't read that one easy," he said to himself, remembering his own heart-bruising time with the book years earlier.

He was surprised to hear the old Land Rover roar in a little after ten, while he was still on the telephone with Georgina telling her about chasing down Chummy King's cows.

"I hear Linny's truck," he said. "Better hang up. See you tomorrow noon then? O.K., love you, honey. Drive careful."

"You want a talk?" he called to Linny, hearing the screen door squeak.

"Yeah, but first I want a read the books and get the background. Then I will know what questions to ask. O.K.?"

"Well," he said. "That makes sense." But he felt a twist of disappointment. His thoughts on the subject had surfaced, his mind like a tongue probing an infected tooth. He wanted to get into the nickel misery of those crushed ancestors, measure his schizoid self against the submerged past.

"You let me know when."

"You bet," she said and pounded up the stairs with the books.

The next morning in the kitchen her face was swollen, both eyes red slits.

"Up all night?"

"Just about." Her voice was rough and cold. She poured a cup of coffee. He asked no more questions.

It was almost a week before they talked. The days had gone by, Linny down in the old building sorting papers and making lists, but at night, instead of heading for the bars she stayed in her room. Georgina said it was a sign the girl was settling down. Charlie thought she was reading the bitter books. On Thursday, Georgina said she had to go up to Sheridan again. There was an important match, some South American polo players of note, a gala dinner.

"I'll stay over with Nora Bible," she said, naming a ranch wife who ran the refreshment tables at all the polo events. "Not so many people bring their picnic baskets like in the old days when it was tailgate city. Don't one a you want a come up for the match? Charlie, you haven't seen one for a year, anyway. Be nice. And, Linny, I bet you never even been to a polo match."

"Oh, I got too many things goin on right here," said Charlie. "Take some snaps for me and tell me about it."

Linny shook her head at Georgina and went upstairs.

The cans of film stood in a row on the dresser. She knew a great deal now about what they might show—an Indian dragging a soldier from a horse, some fake hand-to-hand fighting, Indians poking two white captive women with a stick, the Gatling and Hotchkiss guns spraying, and everywhere Buffalo Bill peering into the distance, riding at the front, his white showman's goatee wriggling in the wind like an albino eel. She did not open any of the cans. She knew also that nothing in the film could possibly equal the tragic power of the single still photograph of Big Foot wrapped in rags lying dead on his back in the snow, his long frozen arms half-raised as if to ward off the bullets, his open ice-glazed eyes fixed forever on anyone who cared to look at him.

Charlie and Linny rinsed the dishes and arranged them in the dishwasher. Charlie never went near the machine without thinking of his mother sloshing chipped plates in an old grey enamel dishpan.

"Dad, can we talk about the Indian stuff now?" She rubbed furiously at the clean counter with a sponge.

"The Indian stuff," he said.

"Yeah. We're Sioux, you always told me, but I don't know what kind a Sioux, and you always said you were born on a rez, but what rez?"

"Oglala Sioux, and I was born at Wazi Ahanhan, Pine Ridge, next a Rosebud. That's where they pushed old Red Cloud's people after they got them out a the Powder River country. That Powder River country was the last a the old, old ways. Red Cloud ought a see it now, all full a methane gas pads and roads."

"So Red Cloud could be a relation? I mean, we could be connected to him, right?"

"We might be."

"Then what are we doin here with this—with Georgina?" She waved at the dishwasher, the poppies in a blue vase on the kitchen table. "Why aren't we with our own people? Don't I got cousins and grandparents and all?"

He'd known these questions would be coming, but the answers were still floating around in the blue sky.

"Linny, I'm sorry, baby girl—I been de-Indianized. I been out workin in the wide world since I was fourteen. The rez didn't have anything for me. And I never kept in touch with any a them." But even as he spoke it was as though he were a tall kettle boiling away and his daughter had just raised the lid. The steam rushed forth. Linny stood there, rigid, brimming with anguish and the sense of isolation that she had breathed in from the books all the week long.

"I bet you never been on a rez, have you?" he said. She shook her head.

"There's more to it than deciding whether you want a live on the rez or in the world. Remember that Indians did not invent the rez. They were the white man's prisons to get the Indians off the good land. Linny, there's no virtue in choosin the rez. You can lock yourself into a corner with no way out."

The girl made an impatient face, little more than a twist of the lips but discounting all he was saying.

He knew it was hopeless but went on. "I'm guessin you want a do the whole thing, don't you—sweat lodge, beaded moccasins, get yourself a pretty Indian name, find a good-lookin Indian stud, and get into the rez life? I see that brain goin a million miles a hour. Just so you know, I had those same feelins long ago. I went back, met your mother, got you started, and so forth. Romance. To me, now, the romance is wherever you find it, but not very likely on a rez."

"Why didn't you guys give me a Indian name?"

"We did." He smiled. "Little Bedbug."

"Dad! Goddammit, I'll pick my own name. Something nice. Like Red Deer or Jade Blossom."

"You got your cultures mixed up."

"Well, what's your name? They didn't name you Charlie, did they?"

"Yeah, they did. They saw how the world was, so they named me Charlie. I suppose you want me to go around bein called Stands Lookin Sideways or Big Dick?"

The girl's face was black-red, and he was afraid she was going to start crying or shouting. But she said, "You wait," and ran up the stairs to her room. In a few seconds she was back again with paper in her hands.

"You can make fun," she said, "but I been readin all that Buffalo Bill Cody stuff in Mr. Brawls' boxes, there, all that stuff about the movie he was goin a make, that he did make, called it *The Indian Wars Refought,* and they staged a couple a the important battles. Most a the movie was the reenactment of Wounded Knee. For the movie Buffalo Bill got all the survivors together, Indians and army soldiers, and had them do it again for the camera. Put himself in as a scout. The books say it was the first documentary. The guns was loaded with blanks and only passed out at the last minute because some a the Indians wanted a use real bullets and shoot the army. General Miles was ridin around orderin everybody do this and do that. It was all very realistic and exact, and guys who'd been there almost passed out when they saw it."

She took a deep breath and looked at him with red-faced sincerity. "The *big* thing is, that movie has totally disappeared and there are people would give a lot a money for that film. There are no copies anywhere. It was only showed a couple a times, then, after Buffalo Bill died in 1917 Essanay gave it another title and started showin it. But nobody paid much attention and now it's lost. There's some think the government got rid of it because it was too realistic, showed the U.S. Army in a bad light shootin women and babies with that big Hotchkiss machine gun cannon."

"No shit! That's the film you found in them little cans?"

"Yeah. Or I think, goin by the labels on the cans. Can't really tell until somebody looks at them."

"Hell, let's go see. Where are they?"

"Dad, we can't do that. They been sealed up in those airtight cans for ninety years. You open those cans and the film will disintegrate right before your eyes. They got to go to a special laboratory specializes in film preservation. Get opened underwater or something."

She rattled the paper. "Anyway, there's a couple reviews in Mr. Brawls' boxes from when it was first showed in 1914 and one guy thought it was the greatest movie ever made and most a them wrote how nothin like it had been ever done before. But I found somebody not so crazy about that movie. They had it at the library in a Buffalo Bill folder. This Chauncey Yellow Robe didn't like Buffalo Bill's movie. He was a Sioux, but it don't say from where."

She stepped forward and by that motion made the kitchen space in front of the counter a stage. She began to recite, her voice deepening, impassioned, and for Charlie Parrott, leaning against the wall, his daughter, eyes narrowed and jaw outthrust, became the long-dead Yellow Robe, speaking with bitter scorn. His hair stirred.

"'You ask how to settle the Indian troubles. I have a suggestion. Let Buffalo Bill and General Miles take some soldiers and go around the reservations and shoot them down. That will settle his troubles. Let them do in earnest what they have been doing at the battlefield at Wounded Knee. These two, who were not even there when it happened, went back and became heroes for a moving picture machine.'"

She had become the old orator, her eyes fixed on Charlie, her right hand extended, shaking, the nail of her index finger a glowing coal. She continued, her voice swollen with Yellow Robe's contempt.

"'You laugh, but my heart does not laugh. Women and children and old men of my people, my relatives, were massacred with machine guns by soldiers of this Christian nation while the fighting men were away. It was *not* a glorious battle, and I should think these two men would be glad they were not there; but no, they want to be heroes for moving pictures. You will be able to see their bravery and their hairbreadth escapes soon in your theatres.'"

She stopped, put her head down, chin on her chest. Gradually she became Linny again.

"Hey, that was scary," said her father. "It felt like old Yellow Robe was right here in the kitchen."

"At least his words were." She spoke in her normal voice. Yellow Robe had gone back into the sky.

But the recitation had moved Charlie Parrott. He wondered if his mother were still alive. A memory of the reservation came unbidden, a blistering day, the sky white and dry, heat waves trembling above the junk cars, one of them where a woman named Mona plied her trade. Nothing moved, no dogs, no people, no lift of wind stirring the dust and trash. He recalled the awful boredom of the place, the hopeless waiting for nothing. He shuddered.

"Tell you what. Soon as Georgina gets back we'll go down there. To Pine Ridge. I'll find out who is still around. You can see for yourself. We'll take that lousy Land Rover a yours—it'll look good on the rez."

"What, today?"

"You bet."

"Georgina will be pissed, a lot a those boxes and papers still got to be done. Because I probably won't come back."

"I know that, but I bet she can hire somebody in town, some college kid finishing out the summer. It's not the end a the world."

"And how about the film cans? Like, they really are valuable. They could be worth a hundred thousand dollars to the right people."

There was a long silence.

"Well. By rights they belong to Georgina. I guess it's your decision what to do with them. Now, what say we get packed up? Georgina comes back I need a talk to her. Maybe an hour."

"What for? Let's just go. Leave her a note."

"Unmannerly. I got a tell her what I'm doin, what the scene is. So she don't worry."

"Goddammit!"

"Linny, grow up. She means somethin a me. I'm not just walkin out without a word. And remember that all you been reading happened a long time ago—more than a hunderd years ago."

"No, Dad. To me it happened last week. I never knew any a that stuff. They don't teach it in school. It gets me—" And she slammed her chest with a theatrical thump.

"You'll have to work it out yourself. We all do." He knew nothing he said would be heard. She would get involved, and after a few years of passionate activism she might fall away from it and end up on urban sidewalks in the company of street chiefs and hookers. He went into the storage room off the kitchen, where she heard him shoving suitcases around.

She understood finally that her father was weak, that all of his choices had been made passively because he let things go and go and go, waiting until situations crested, until the move was made for him. Her mother had left him, made her own way. He had ended up working on ranches even though he was smart because he didn't have any ambition. She bet Georgina had picked him and he'd just gone along with it. She bit at her nails, an old habit from childhood. He was the classic irresponsible, passive guy, no Crazy Horse or Sitting Bull fired with resistance, but letting the whites push him around, believing that he had some kind of decent life. And, she believed, he couldn't stand to kiss Georgina's money goodbye—probably his last chance at real money, seeing he was in his forties. She despised his weakness but didn't blame him. She would let him take her around the rez, introduce the relatives, and then he could go back to Georgina and the money. She'd find out the rest of it by herself.

She packed rapidly, sorting through her clothes, cramming the short skirts and halter tops into the wastebasket. She was through with those clothes. She pulled on jeans and an overlarge T-shirt as long as a nightgown. She heard Georgina's car pull up outside, the kitchen door slam, and the rumble of her father's voice. The duffel bags were full. She was ready. Downstairs she heard the freezer door open and shut. She guessed Charlie was mixing Georgina a drink. He himself never drank. His voice rose and fell. What was he telling Georgina? The woman could never understand any of this. Linny sat on the edge of the bed and waited.

After a long time her father's voice ballooned up the stairwell. "Linny! You ready? Let's roll."

She dragged the duffel bags out onto the landing and kicked them down the stairs.

"O.K.," she yelled. "Great."

She took three steps down, then turned and rushed back to the bedroom. The cans of film sat on the dresser. It was difficult getting the lids off the first two. Inside the first one the coils of old nitrate film were clotted and welded together in a solid mass. The next deteriorated before her eyes to nitrate dandruff. She knocked one film out onto the bed. It had a nasty smell, and as it uncoiled and broke apart she could see that the center of each frame had been burned through by the acidic gases that had attacked the emulsion.

Then she was down the stairs, dragging the duffel bags.

"Bye," she called to Georgina, who stood on the porch, face expressionless, staring at Charlie.

As they pulled out onto the main road he said, "What did you do about the film?"

"Oh, I left it for her."

"Good girl," he said, and he patted her still unwounded knee.

The Trickle Down Effect

DEB SIPPLE HAD HAD IT BOTH WAYS—EASY AND HARD.
It had been easy when he was a kid lording it over his two
sisters, enjoying the run of the ranch he'd believed would someday be his, getting first pick of the horses, hacking chunks off the
don't-touch devil's food cake the cook had made for dinner. But
as he moved into his mid-twenties the easy edges fell off. The
ranch had gone to the Elk Tooth bank, his sisters lived in Oregon,
there were no more good horses left, and he'd developed an
allergy to chocolate. In a search for the famous solace of open
spaces he'd built up a drinking habit. By the weary age of thirty
he'd been married twice, and it hadn't taken permanently either
time despite the fact that he had small feet and a big pecker.
Modern women had different standards than their grandmothers.
Both wives had named alcohol abuse and Deb's lack of steady
income as crucial factors in the breakups. He smoked, too, but not
much was made of that. Jeanine called him a sorry shit; Paula cried
large round tears, said she loved him still but would be leaving
him for a sheep rancher the coming weekend.

"What. You are runnin off with some mangy sheepherder."

"Not a sheepherder. Rancher. He owns a sheep ranch."

"Sure he does. And if you are goin, don't do me no favors to
wait for the weekend, get the hell out *right now*." And he helped

her pack by throwing her clothes, makeup pots and jars, sewing machine, and other female accoutrements into the yard.

Deb's only asset was his flatbed truck. Most of what little money he made with occasional hauling funneled straight into Elk Tooth's three bars, what bartender Amanda Gribb called the Wyoming trickle down effect. He would run up a big tab at the Pee Wee, and when Amanda leaned on him he switched to the Silvertip and the Pee Wee saw him not. When the Silvertip debt began to be mentioned he favored Muddy's Hole and dropped hints that he was looking for a job or two. Everyone understood that he wasn't interested in a real job but in a few days' work. Sooner or later something came up, and when he collected he'd hit the Pee Wee, pay off his tab, and start a new one. So went the cycle of Deb Sipple's years measured in bar bills and small work.

Wyoming had been dry as a quart of sand for three years and Elk Tooth was in the heart of the drought disaster zone. Those ranchers who had held on to their herds hoping for rain were caught like mice. As the summer drew to its stove-lid end, the most precious commodity to those in the cow business was hay, and the prices demanded for it matched the prices for rubies. Ranchers spent hours on the telephone and searching the Internet for reasonably priced hay. No flimsy or wild rumor could be ignored. If a rancher heard of hay up in Saskatchewan that a seller described simply as "not moldy" she'd try for it.

Most of the desperate ranchers were women, for in Elk Tooth lady ranchers abound, some who had stepped into ownership when a husband rancher died, some the mature daughters of men who had sired no male heirs, some ex-CEOs who had tossed up everything and headed for the high country, as close to Jackson as they could get.

One of the ranchers was Fiesta Punch, a good horsewoman,

but rough on the hired help. She ran Red Cheerios, a weird brand of exotics with white rings around their eyes her grandfather had bred up, but this summer their range was so badly gnawed it resembled the surface of an antique billiard table in an attic heavily populated by moths. There was no point in selling. The market was glutted and prices lower than breakeven. And she wanted to hold on to what was probably the only herd of Red Cheerios in existence. She had to get her hands on enough hay to carry them through the fall and winter. She owed that much to family heritage.

The double trouble with scarce hay was that in addition to paying through the nose for the stuff, when she finally located some, she would have to face fearsome transport charges. The only decent hay grew in distant parts, and hay transporters knew a penned turkey when they saw one. Hauling the hay from Farmer X to Rancher Z could double the cost of the precious bales. Fiesta Punch was in a position to lose her shirt. On the other pan of the scale Deb Sipple, with his big flatbed truck, could almost guarantee himself several years of elbow security at the Pee Wee.

Ms. Punch was hunched over her account books one night alternately adding figures and cracking her knuckles when the phone rang.

"Fiesta?"

"Yes."

"You don't know me but this is the friend of a friend."

"Friend of a friend?" She could hear country and western music—Dwight Yoakam's rock-drill voice—in the background. "What is it? You want to talk about urban legends?"

"What?"

"Never mind. What can I do for you? I'm kind a busy."

"I know where you can git you some hay. Good hay."

"Where might that be? Shangsi Province? The Upper Volta region?"

"No, just up there in Westconston. I got a friend in Cooke City and his cousin Björn got hay. It's not so drouthy up there."

"Two or three bales, right?"

"Wrong. He got eighty bales. Them big round ones, them thousand-pound ones you need a bale fork to lift."

"Let me see if I got this straight. Your friend is in Cooke City, Montana, and his cousin with the hay is in Wisconsin."

"Uh-huh."

"What kind a money does he want for it?" Wisconsin hay was expensive.

The caller named a ridiculously low figure, seventy dollars a ton, the cost of hay three years earlier.

"Must be full a weeds and thistles."

"It's good hay. You can drive up there, look at it. But you better be fast, he won't have it long. So far you're the only one knows about it." He gave her Björn's phone number in Disk, Wisconsin.

"So how come I'm the lucky rancher gets to hear about this great hay?" she said, but her question fell on a dead connection.

She flew up to La Crosse, rented the airport's last available car, and drove out to Disk. Björn Smith was a thready blond in his forties with a round head and beaky orange nose that gave him the look of a seagull. He showed her the hay, stowed in a capacious, fragrant barn. It was prime alfalfa hay, holding green. She pulled out a handful and looked at it—there was a high proportion of leaf to stem, it was pliable and clean. She noticed it had been cut when in the bud stage. There was nothing like Wisconsin alfalfa hay.

"First cutting?" she asked.

Björn nodded. "I could a sold it at the hay auction for more but

Deb said you was a friend and needed hay bad. I guess you got a mean drought over there in Wyoming?"

She twisted her mouth in sardonic agreement, paid him on the spot. There goes almost six grand, she thought.

"I'll get Deb come pick it up soon's I can," she said, folding the bill of sale into her wallet.

"Sooner the better. I want a get out a here."

"Givin up farmin?"

"Yeah. Goin a film school at UCLA."

"No kiddin. Like learnin how to make movies?"

"That's right. I got ideas."

"Oh," said Fiesta Punch, "we all got *them*." Then, more kindly, "I hope you make it."

Deb Sipple was in Muddy's Hole cutting the dust with his eleventh beer and seventh cigarette when Fiesta Punch came through the door and looked around, headed for him as if following a chalk line drawn across the floor.

"Hello, Deb. That's a filthy habit. Everbody else but you give up smokin. Anyways, I bought some hay up in Wisconsin and I want you to go pick it up as soon as possible. Tomorrow."

"West*cons*ton! Hell, that's halfway across the country. That's the other side a the Mississippi. It's almost in New York."

"Not quite. It's in Disk, just over the Iowa line. As I think you know, so don't play dumb." She knew who the anonymous caller had been. "Speed is necessary. Your pal Björn wants to split and I need the hay. It's a couple trips for you."

He put on a sly face. "You know I'm goin a bite your red rosy ass with a heavy price."

"That's what I come to discuss."

"I got to ask two dollars fifty a ton."

"I'll take it!" She could hardly believe her ears. She had been expecting to hear twenty or thirty dollars per ton.

"Per mile," said Deb Sipple.

Fiesta Punch figured the damage rapidly. It was give or take nine hundred miles to Disk, Wisconsin. Eighty tons times two dollars and fifty cents was two hundred dollars per mile times give or take nine hundred miles was—no way.

"That's what I call a highway holdup. That's over a hunderd eighty thousand dollars. That's more'n the herd's worth. I guess the spirit a Butch Cassidy ain't dead yet."

"Fiesta, you could drive up there yourself in your pickup, bring it back a ton at a time. Or you could rent one a them U-Hauls. Shouldn't take you more'n a few weeks a git her done if you work at it steady."

"You know I can't do that. I got responsibilities here. I got bovines need lookin after. Tell you what, I'll pay you fifty dollars a ton and no mileage charge. It comes to about four grand. I can afford that, just barely, and you will make out like a pig in a feather bed."

"Oink, oink," said Deb Sipple. "Make it five." Fiesta Punch nodded grimly.

Someone put money in the jukebox, and Dwight Yoakam began to sing.

The first trip was easy. Deb Sipple drank a beer with Björn, had the truck loaded and secured in two hours, the hay bales lined up to make two huge cylinders. On the way back he took a northern route, stopped in Albert Lea, Minnesota, a town whose crimson past has faded to pink but where Deb Sipple had no trouble finding the Electric Silo, a honky-tonk where he took on some personal freight that gave him a bad headache by 4:00 a.m. In South Dakota he stopped for four cups of coffee and a bison steak and, after a cigarette and a piece of apple pie, was feeling well enough to continue. Fiesta Punch had him unload the hay in the pasture near her main gate.

"I'll pay you for the whole run when you bring the second load," she said, then relented under the force of his pitiable pleading and paid him a hundred on account.

The second trip was notable in every way. He got off to a bad start by picking up a female hitchhiker who told him she'd been in prison in Florida with Aileen Wuornos, the serial killer, whom she counted as her best friend. He made an excuse to stop at a service station and when, at his suggestion, she got out to use the ladies' room, he took off. To steady his nerves he visited Albert Lea again and so missed the weather report warning of windstorms in the coming days, and when he pulled into Björn's it was well past midnight. The hay man was not pleased and told him to sleep in his truck until daylight.

It was noon before he woke up. It took four hours to load the hay, partly because the wind was gusting to sixty, partly because Deb Sipple was distracted to find he had smoked all his cigarettes in Albert Lea and his host laughed cruelly when he asked for tobacco. Then he discovered he had forgotten to bring the tarp.

"What the hell, it gets wet it gets wet, right?"

It is no fun to drive a big rig loaded with round hay bales under a dark sky in high wind with a hangover and the cigarette fits, but that's how it was for Deb Sipple. When once again he came to Albert Lea it was nightfall and natural to pull into the Electric Silo, a bar he ranked second only to the Pee Wee. He thought briefly about moving to Minnesota. He apologized to the comely bar girl (who remembered him by name) for drinking only four beers,

explained that he was in a hurry, bought three packs of cigarettes for the road, and said good night. Outside the wind had
lessened a little and he could see something like stars overhead.
The weather was clearing.

But the scanty number of beers left him with a gnawing,
unsatisfied feeling, and in Rapid City he found Klipper's Klip
Joint, which had everything he wanted, from cheap shots to
foaming on-tap to Dwight Yoakam songs. At some point two men
carried him out to his truck and heaved him up into the seat, told
him to sleep it off. But hardly had they gone back inside than he
was bolt upright behind the wheel and fumbling for his cigarettes.
A cigarette going, it was only natural to start up and drive, and in
half an hour he'd found his way out of Rapid City with its crazy
double street lamps and whirling traffic lights and was sailing west
on I-90. The minute he hit the Wyoming line he felt better,
opened the third pack, and lit another cigarette to celebrate a
return to his home state. It was a jolt to find he already had a cigarette going, but he threw the half-smoked one out the window
and rolled on. He got off the interstate as soon as he could, dimly
aware that it would not be the best time for a conversation with a
state trooper. By the time he turned onto the road for Sack, with
Elk Tooth only forty miles beyond, he had tossed fourteen burning cigarettes out the window and many of them had nuzzled into
hay bales.

Deb Sipple's return was the closest thing to a meteor ever seen
in Elk Tooth, his truck a great fiery cylinder hurtling through
the darkness. Those who missed seeing it have to depend on
the reports of the fortunate few who were awake at that hour. The
most vivid account will come from Fiesta Punch, who lost not
only the burned cargo but the bales he'd delivered earlier, con-

sumed in the myriad grass fires that followed him into town and laid waste the ranch country. The hundred-dollar bill Deb had begged from Fiesta Punch had gone to gasoline and the Electric Silo.

"I guess they're even," said Amanda Gribb.

What Kind of Furniture Would Jesus Pick?

S AILING THE SAGEBRUSH OCEAN, A TRAVELER DISCOVERS isolated coves with trophy houses protected by electronic gates, or slanted trailers on waste ground, teetering rock formations and tilted cliffs, log houses unchanged from the nineteenth century except for the television dish.

The Harp Ranch was one of eight or nine spreads in a small basin east of the Big Horns. All of these places had been cut from the holdings of a big Scots outfit that pulled out in 1897. Budgel Wolfscale, a telegraph clerk from Missouri, on his way to Montana to search for the yellow metal, stopped at a Wyoming road ranch for a supper of fried venison and coffee, heard there was good range. For the next week he rode around the country, finally staked a homestead claim where Scots cows had spent their brief time.

A year-round stream, Bull Jump Creek, cut the property, fringed by cottonwoods and willows, the shining maroon branches of water birch. It was still open country, though barbwire was coming in with the nesters. He built a shotgun cabin of hauled-out lodgepole, married one of the girls from a distant Ham's Fork whorehouse, and naming the ranch after the harp his mother had played, thought himself a Wyoming rancher. He wasn't that, but his sons and grandsons were.

The Harp skidded down the generations to Gilbert Wolfscale, born on the ranch in 1945, and still living a son's life with his mother in the old house that had been gradually enlarged with telescoped additions until the structure resembled a giant spyglass built of logs. He ran a cow-calf operation, usually worked the place alone for even inept help was hard to find. He was a tall man with heavy bones. His coarse skin seemed made of old leather upholstery, and instead of lips, a small seam opened and disclosed his cement-colored teeth. There were no horses that could match his stamina. Despite his muscle mass he moved with fluid quickness. He surrounded himself with an atmosphere of affronted hostility as if he'd just been insulted, but balanced it with a wild and boisterous laugh, which erupted at inappropriate times. He was addicted to what he called "hammer coffee," strong enough to dissolve the handle, float the head.

The old world was gone, he knew that. For some reason a day in the 1950s when all the ranchers and their hands had worked on the road rose often in his mind and with such vividness that he could smell the mud, the mineral odor of wet rock. It had been the last rainy spring before that decade's drought sucked the marrow out of the state. The county road that ran between Kingring and Sheridan passed through seven ranches over a fifty-mile stretch. Under heavy melt from the mountains the road went to quagmire, became an impassable sump of greasy mud and standing water. The county had no money. The ranchers threw logs and scrap wood into the deepest ruts, but they sank out of sight in minutes. Some of the holes were three feet deep. If the ranchers wanted to get to town they would have to fix it themselves or wait until it dried. On a drizzling morning in April his father drank his coffee standing up.

"What say, Gib? Want to come along?"

They rode together on Butch, his father's roan saddle mount. As they rode the rain stopped but heavy clouds moved with the bumping wind. Gilbert clutched the lard pail that held their lunch. They came to a place where men with shovels were strung out along the road. There was a section of an old corral still standing near the road, and here men had leaned their tools, lunch pails, and bottles. A few had thrown down their jackets on the ground. His father tethered Butch to a post.

While the men cleaned the borrow ditches and culverts, cut new drainage channels, built water bars, and hauled gravel, Gilbert hacked manfully at the mud with a broken hoe, but he went to the weathered corral to play with sticks and rocks when Old Man Bunner told him to get out of his way or he'd chop off his legs. The rocks were wet. He built a play corral of mud and broken miner's candle stems, and inside placed the rocks which were his horses. The wind cleared out the weather, and by noon it was broken blue sky.

"Warmin up," called one of the men, stretching his back. The sun shone behind his ears, which turned the color of chokecherry jelly.

The lunch of cold pork and boiled eggs seemed the best thing Gilbert had ever eaten. There were two squares of his mother's coarse white cake with peanut butter icing at the bottom of the pail. His father said Gilbert could have both pieces. He fell asleep on the way home, rocked by Butch's easy walk. His mother groaned with rage when she saw the mud on his clothes. The next morning his father went to work on the road without him and he cried until his mother slapped him and told him to shut up. The work went on for a week, and when it ended a truck could get over the road. The first time they drove past the place he looked for his play corral. He could see one miner's candle stem. The rest had blown away. The rock horses were still there. Fifty years later the road was graveled and graded by the county, but he still looked when he drove past the place, the old corral now nothing but a single post. The prairie had swallowed his horse rocks.

*　*　*

After Gilbert Wolfscale inherited the ranch he enlarged the two irrigated alfalfa fields, which made it possible, in bad years, to feed the cattle through the winter, and in good years to sell hay to less fortunate outfits. These two fields kept the ledger ink black. He came up with ideas to increase the income. He thought of butchering and packing the beef himself to bypass the middlemen, who took the money while the rancher did the work, but the local stores preferred to stay with the chain suppliers. So he started his own butcher shop and built a refrigerated slaughterhouse with storage facility. He put an ad in the paper looking for private customers and found half a dozen, but they didn't eat enough beef to make the venture pay and a woman from town complained that there were bone splinters in the ground beef. He raised turkeys, thinking surefire Thanksgiving and Christmas markets, but never sold very many, even when he put strings of cranberries around their necks. His mother spent days making the cranberry neck-laces, but people wanted the plastic-wrapped, prebasted Safe-way turkeys with breasts like Las Vegas strippers. They ate the turkeys themselves, his mother canning most of the meat. They were sick of the smell of turkey soup by spring.

Some of the original chock-and-log fence—built not of split rails or slender poles but big logs—still stood in the high pastures nearest the forest, but much had been replaced with five-strand barbwire. He could almost see the ground compressing under the heavy log weight. How many men had helped his grandfather put up that fence of entire tree trunks? Gilbert put in his time work-ing on the barb fences, which no longer had the tensile strength of fresh wire but were patched and mended with short lengths of various gauge. In an earlier decade, struggling to finish the job on a hot afternoon, he had cast about for a stick or something to twist tight a diagonal cross-brace wire, but the only thing at hand was a cow's bleached leg bone with its useful trochlea head, which seemed made to jam fence wire tight. It worked so well that he collected and used cow bones in dozens of places. These bony fences and the coyote skulls nailed to the corner posts gave the Harp a murderous air.

He was a model of rancher stubbornness, savagely possessive of his property. He did everything in an odd, deliberate way, Gilbert Wolfscale's way, and never retreated once he had taken a position. Neighbors said he was self-reliant, but there was a way they said it that meant something else.

Seven miles north of the Harp on the Stump Hole Road lived May and Jim Codenhead of his generation. He had gone to grade school with May—she was then May Alwen—in the old century during the postwar fifties, the Eisenhower era of interstate highway construction that changed Wyoming forever by letting in the outside. May's brother, Sedley Alwen, a big, good-natured kid with stringy arms, had been Gilbert's best friend. Gilbert courted May for a year, had taken it for granted that Sedley would be his brother-in-law, but she strung him along and then, in a sudden move on Christmas Day in 1966, married Jim Codenhead. Jim was then nothing more than an illiterate Montana hand working on the Alwen place. May taught him to read until he could fumble through the newspaper.

"That's the shits, man," said Sedley sympathetically and took Gilbert on a two-day drunk that was as much a salute to his draft notice as balm for Gilbert's disappointment.

The marriage wasn't unprecedented. For those who took the long view and had patience, it was the classic route for a lowly cowhand to own his own spread—marry the rancher's daughter. In retaliation Gilbert went to a New Year's dance, found Suzzy New, and in ten days pressured her into a fast marriage.

Suzzy New was slender and small-boned, something French about her child-size wrists, a contrast to Gilbert, six foot four, bullnecked with heavy shoulders. She was nimble-fingered and a talented embroiderer. In the flush of their first months together Gilbert bragged that she was so handy she could make a pair of chaps for a hummingbird. She was quiet, disliked arguments and shouting. She held herself tensely and had a way of retreating into her thoughts. She believed herself to be a very private person. She slept badly, sensitive to the slightest abnormal sound—the creak of an attic timber, the rising wind, a raccoon forcing its way through the skirting of the house and under the kitchen floorboards. She had let herself be bullied into marrying Gilbert, and within days of the ruinous act bitterly regretted it.

All her life she had heard and felt the Wyoming wind and took it for granted. There had even been a day when she was a young girl standing by the road waiting for the school bus when a spring wind, fresh and warm and perfumed with pine resin, had caused a bolt of wild happiness to surge through her, its liveliness promising glinting chances. She had loved the wind that day. But out at the ranch it was different and she became aware of moving air's erratic, inimical character. The house lay directly in line with a gap in the encircling hills to the northwest, and through this notch the prevailing wind poured, falling on the house with ferocity. The house shuddered as the wind punched it, slid along its sides like a released torrent from a broken dam. Week after week in winter it sank and rose, attacked and feinted. When she put her head down and went out to the truck, it yanked at her clothing, shot up her sleeves, whisked her hair into raveled fright wigs. Gilbert seemed not to notice, but then, she thought, he probably regarded it as *his* wind, and no doubt took pleasure in such a powerful possession.

*　　*　　*

Sedley went to Vietnam. Gilbert, who had a growth inside his nose, was 4-F despite his strength and muscle. Sedley was captured by the Vietcong and spent several years in a bamboo cage. He came back a different person, crisscrossed with sudden rages brought on by inconsequential events, such as the rattle of dishes or a truck crossing the bridge. He was thought to be unstable and in need of watchful care. He moved in with May and Jim. May could calm Sedley down when he was having one of his fits. She had always been close to Sedley, had, from the time she was a small child with nightmares, padded down the hall and into his moonless north room, climbed into his bed for warmth and protection. The infant she bore six months after she married Jim Codenhead might have been her brother's child or, for that matter, Gilbert Wolfscale's or even Jim Codenhead's. For years, whenever Gilbert was at their house, he studied the child, Patty, trying to work out whom she resembled. He could come to no conclusion.

Vietnam nightmares tortured Sedley Alwen. Sometimes, to give May a break, Gilbert made the long drive, taking him to Cheyenne to the Veterans Administration hospital, where Sedley saw the shrink and got his prescriptions renewed. It was a two-day trip and they stayed in a motel overnight, sharing a room. After the session Sedley would be talkative and excited. Gilbert listened attentively to his stories of torture and comrades' deaths. It was at these times Sedley resembled the friend of his childhood, excited and eager, though the subject matter was fearful. But he could not have whiskey. They tried it once and found out. Whiskey made him act up, smashing the motel furniture and howling at the light fixture in the ceiling.

By the end of the century Gilbert was fifty-five and caught in the downward ranching spiral of too much work, not enough money, drought. It kept getting drier and drier, grasshoppers appearing as early as April and promising a plague in August. The grass crackled like eggshells under his feet. There was no color in the landscape, the alkali dust muting sage, grass, stones, the earth itself. When a vehicle passed along the road a fine cloud spread out and slowly settled. The air was baked of scent except for the chalky dust with its faint odor of old cardboard. He was conscious of how many things could go wrong, of how poorly he'd reckoned the ranch's problems.

To the new-moneyed suitcase ranchers who had moved in all around him—ex-California real estate agents, fabulous doctors, and retired cola executives—the Harp looked a skanky, run-down outfit. They noticed the yard littered with stacks of rusted sheet metal held down by railroad ties, a pile of crooked fence posts inhabited by chipmunks, the long string of log additions to the old house. Some of these rich people, heated with land fever and the thought of a bargain, came to Gilbert and offered to buy his ranch. He could see in their eyes how they planned to bulldoze the house and build mansions with guest cottages. Guest cottages seemed reprehensible to him.

"Them rich pricks are lower than a snake's ass in a wagon track," he said to his mother. "I told him, my granddad homesteaded this place and if I ever seen his California butt on my property again I'd shoot it off. I looked him right in the eye and he got the message. He turned color so fast he farted."

His mother produced her hard little laugh.

It had always been dry country, and no one born there expected more than a foot of annual rainfall in a good year. The drought halved that, and he could see the metamorphosis of grazing land into desert. The country wanted to go to sand dunes and rattlesnakes, wanted to scrape off its human ticks. The shortage of grass and hay forced him to cut back on his cattle. He didn't have enough hay to feed his own stock. Everything told him that the day of the rancher was fading, but he dodged admitting it. He blamed the government, he blamed Salt Lake City, for the damn Mormons, he said, had seeded the clouds for the Olympics, sucking out all the snow moisture before it reached Wyoming. The ranch house well was eleven hundred feet deep and the water brackish. In the drought years of the 1930s and again in the '50s, his father had put in earthen dams and stock ponds, and in wet years they had held water but now were silted up and dried and stood as unsightly pits filled with weeds. In the center of one dry hole he piled an immense stack of dry brush, adding more every year, intending to burn it with the first good snow.

He was pestered. Some newcomer wanted a shortcut easement through the ranch to his million-dollar luxury house on the other side. A long-nosed Game & Fish biologist nagged him about fences that blocked antelope passage. Hunters wanted to shoot his deer. A busybody woman straight out of agricultural school came from the Extension Service one day and lectured him about protecting stream banks from cow-hoof erosion, about pasture rotation to prevent overgrazing.

"I heard all that shit. But I'll tell you what. I let the cows graze where they want and drink where they will. Been doin this for a while. Guess I know somethin about it." He stood in a truculent posture, legs apart, chin thrust forward. The woman shrugged and left.

Although he now lived a bachelor son's life, he knew how it was to be married. His wife, Suzzy, had left him in the spring of 1977 to live in Sheridan, sixty miles distant, when the two boys, Monty and Rod, were still young. Those boys were doomed, said

Gilbert, smacking his hand on the table for emphasis, to grow up without a father's guidance and example, injured because they were denied a boy's life on the ranch.

"If he wants a see the kids why can't he just come into town?" Suzzy said to her mother on the phone after the split. Her voice rose, clipped and complaining. "You know I put in years on that ranch, and nothin really worked right. Half the time there wasn't water and when there was water it was nasty. We couldn't get in or out in the winter. No telephone, no electricity, no neighbors, his mother always naggin, and the *work*! He wore me down. 'Do this, do that,' bullyin ways. Keep that old house clean? Couldn't be done. He could a sold the place fifty times over and lived decent if he got a job like a normal human bein, but would he? No. I wouldn't relive those years for nothin." Once she had made up her mind to leave, her own stubbornness emerged. But Gilbert refused to agree to a divorce, and the separation and enmity dragged on.

In town she got a cash register job at the Big Boy supermarket, and as soon as the two boys were old enough to run errands and deliver papers she made them get after-school and weekend jobs as well. She was interested in money and showed them there were better things than cows and debt.

The Big Boy job was no good. Not only was the pay low but she disliked having to repeat "Have a nice day" to people who deserved to be ridden bareback by the devil wearing can openers for spurs, and one day she quit to take a job as a filing clerk in the county treasurer's office. It graveled Gilbert that she handled his property tax and vehicle registration papers.

She wore him down on the divorce, and he gave up after a fight in town in her new house. She had bought an old brick mansion with big trees in the yard and an iron ornamental fence around it. In the 1880s the house had belonged to a Chicago merchant who used it two or three times a year to oversee his ranch investments. Gilbert did not understand how she could afford this house. They had argued, then screamed. Gilbert stood with his legs apart and his arms hanging loose. Another man would have recognized this as a bad sign, but she could not stop blaming him, and he, goaded to violence, slapped her a good one and she came at him and yanked out a clump of his hair in the front where it would show, ran to the back of the house, and called the sheriff. When the law came she accused him of assault, showing the red mark on her cheek as proof.

"What about *this*?" shouted Gilbert, pointing to his bleeding scalp, but Sheriff Brant Smich, his second cousin, ignored him. When the divorce finally came through it was settled that if he wanted the boys to help out on the ranch for a weekend he would have to drive in and fetch them and he would have to pay them for their labor. He had paid practically nothing for child support during the long separation, she said, it was the least he could do. He protested, said he had canceled checks to prove he had certainly paid adequate if not luxurious support.

"Take it to court," she said, "you think you been treated so bad."

Neither of the boys came willingly to the ranch. They appeared only in times of crisis after Gilbert telephoned Suzzy, demanding their help—spring branding, fence work. They let themselves be dragged out for a weekend then, sulky and grudging. They sassed their grandmother and whispered and snickered when they saw cows bulling. They only wanted to ride the horses. A day's work was not in them. It was clear to Gilbert that at his death they would sell the place as fast as they could. One day someone would find his stiff corpse out in the pasture, the wire cutters in his hand, or fallen in the muddy irrigation ditch as he had found his own father in 1958. He would never be able to pass on how he felt about the land to them. And this was Suzzy's fault, for she had taken them from him and from the ranch.

His allegiance to the place was not much of a secret, for even outsiders perceived dimly his scalding passion for the ranch, the place he had lived all his years. His possessive gaze fell on the pale teeth of distant mountains, on the gullies and washes, the long draw shedding Indian scrapers and arrowheads. His feeling for the ranch was the strongest emotion that had ever moved him, a strangling love tattooed on his heart. It was his. It was as if he had drunk from some magic goblet brimming with the elixir of ownership. And although the margins of Bull Jump Creek had been trampled bare and muddy by generations of cows, although there were only one or two places along it still flushed with green willow, the destruction had happened so gradually he had not noticed, for he thought of the ranch as timeless and unchanging in its beauty. It needed only young men to put it right. So his thoughts turned again and again on ways to get his sons to see and love the ranch.

In 1982 Monty was fourteen and Rod two years younger. Gilbert, waiting in the truck in front of Suzzy's house, heard Monty inside bellowing at his mother in his cracking voice, "I don't want a go. It stinks out there, there's nothin a do," and he could not dodge the fact that his sons hated the ranch. Somehow they had escaped the scorching obsession of land ownership, and he faulted them for it. In a desperate attempt to make the place more attractive to them he had the power company run out poles and wires, a terrible expense and useless, too, as the boys came no oftener. The only benefit, if benefit it was, was the small television set he bought and put in the living room, where he would lie on the sofa under one of his mother's quilts and watch men wrestling anacondas, riding motorcycles around inside enormous wooden barrels. His mother liked the television, but claimed to be shocked by much of what she saw.

"It is company, I'll say that, but where they find them fool people to cut up so I don't know."

*   *   *

He wasn't lonely. There was his mother, he was a church deacon, a member of the Cattlemen's Association, he went to his neighbors' potluck suppers and barbecues, and about once a month drove to town and got half-drunk, bought a woman, and made it back to the ranch before the old haymaker cleared the horizon. He was not a veteran but he knew all those who were and often went to the VFW with them to drink and listen to the Vietnam stories.

He had always taken an interest in Vietnam. No one was more attentive to war stories. He wondered what it was about combat that so changed men, for all of those who had been in school with him, the ones who came back, were marked in different ways by what they had seen and endured. He knew them and he didn't know them. Sedley came back angry and crazy; Russ Fleshman returned as a windbag; Pete Kitchen was reclusive and lived in a horse trailer at the back of the old Kitchen ranch. Something had gone wrong for Willis McNitt, leaving him dead-voiced and troubled. They all referred emotionally to the war, now so many years past, and Fleshman sometimes put his face in his hands and cried. And there were the ones who didn't come back: Todd Likwartz, Howard Marr, and several men he hadn't known. When he thought of them a phrase came into his mind—"Now they know what Rhamses knows." His mother belonged to the generation that memorized poems in school, and one, "Little Mattie," on the death of a thirteen-year-old girl, had fastened itself relentlessly in her recall with the tolling line "Now she knows what Rhamses knows." She quoted from it through her life and still sometimes treated her son to a recitation of the entire piece with the stilted emphases learned so long ago in a little Wyoming schoolhouse.

Gilbert Wolfscale listened to the veterans. He wanted to understand what he had missed. It was the great experience of the time of his young manhood and he had been absent. It was as though the veterans had learned a different language, he thought, listening to Fleshman's scattershot of *didi mau,* Agent Orange, *beaucoup,* Jodies, 105s, Willy Petes, and K-Bars. He caught at the names—Phu Bai, Khe Sanh, Quang Tri—wondering if these were the Vietnamese equivalents of Rawlins or Thermopolis. The veterans did not seem so much tragic victims as eccentric members of a select club. He felt himself an outsider. They had got the edge on him.

Willis McNitt sat behind him at the August rodeo. It was the hottest summer he had ever known. The horses were blowing and their coats white with salty sweat, the bulls stood in the chutes with their heads down and bucked feebly. There had been a freak accident at the stock pens. The rodeo grounds were old, put up in the 1930s, all wood fence and posts, and somehow a kid watering the roping calves had fallen or been knocked down and mashed his face against a splintery post. A long sliver had run into the flesh below his eyebrow and he had stumbled away from the pens, blood coursing down the back of his hand, which he put to the wound instinctively. He had not cried out, just stumbled into sight with blood seeping between his fingers, making the crowd gasp. As the ambulance bore him away Gilbert said to no one in particular, "They ought a tear out them damn old wood posts and get good metal."

"I seen somethin like that in Nam," said Willis behind him in the flat, heavy voice. Willis had a son at university studying anthropology. The kid—"Coot" McNitt—had a half-baked theory that rice cultivation developed to replace a shortage of maggots in early man's diet. If you listened to him long enough he'd make you believe it. "We was in a fire-free zone and the kid next a me got shot in the eye. He said, 'I been shot in the eye,' said it five or six times, real quiet, like he couldn't quite take it in. Couldn't believe it. Then he laid down beside me and commenced a kick and thrash and ever time he kicked the blood pumped up through his eye like a school water fountain."

"God," said Gilbert. "Did he—?"

"Died. A kid, eighteen years old, younger'n Coot. Couldn't believe he'd been shot. I was nineteen but after that I felt like a old man."

"You ain't old, Willis. Hell, you're my age."

"Yeah." The word dropped like a stone.

In 1999 Gilbert Wolfscale's mother opened an official-looking letter from the California State Allocation Department. She read that she had inherited a sum of money from someone in that state. All she had to do was fill out the enclosed form, mail it back, and in six or eight weeks she would receive the inheritance. She spent two hours filling out the form with its demands for address, social security number, date of birth, bank account numbers, and other tedious details. She sat so long at the table with this form that her left leg went to sleep, and when she got up to go to the kitchen and make a cup of tea it buckled. She fell and broke her hip.

She recuperated very slowly. Even after the break had healed Gilbert had to drive her in weekly to Sheridan for therapy. He sometimes wondered why she didn't get one of her friends to drive her in. She was always on the phone gabbing with her cronies, and most of them still drove. He heard her talking with them about football, which she watched avidly on the television.

"I'm for them Bears. I couldn't never be for them Packers."

When he asked her why she did not arrange a trip to town with Luce or Florence or Helen she said, "They're not family. Suppose the doctor was to give me bad news. I'd want a be with blood kin, not some other person."

While she met with the therapist Gilbert walked around the windy town streets rather than sit in a plastic chair in the stuffy waiting room. In a music store he looked at CDs, wondering at the proliferation of bands with trendy, foolish names. Behind a stiff plastic divider labeled "Miscellaneous" he found birdcalls, tap dancing, the whistles of steam locomotives from around the world. The last CD was *Remembering Vietnam*. The cover showed a grimy infantryman staring up at a helicopter. The back copy listed "Firefight," "Shrapnel," "AFVN," "Jungle Patrol," "Rain," "APC Convoy." He bought it.

In the truck driving home his mother said, "I don't have to go back there but a few more times, looks like, and thanks to heaven. Some a the strangest people settin in that waitin room. These two women got talkin about their Bible class. Sounded pretty modern, you know, tryin a link the Bible to nowadays. But this Bible class *they* went to was tryin a guess how it would be if Jesus showed up in Sheridan. That got them all excited and there they set, what would he do for work. They both said he could easy find a job workin construction. Would he have his own house and would it be like a trailer or a regular house or a apartment? Then they got at the furniture, what kind a furniture would Jesus pick for his place. And you know how you get thinkin about things you overhear? Wasn't none a my business but there I set, crazy as they was, wonderin if he'd pick out a maple rockin chair or a sofa with that Scotchgard fabric or what."

A month before his mother's fall she had bought some brightly colored kitchen sponges. One of them was purple, and she had developed an affection for it, never using it on greasy pots or to wipe up nasty spills. He dribbled coffee on the counter one morning and began to mop at the spill with the distinguished sponge.

"What are you doin! Don't use that—take the pink one. You dunderhead, I'm savin that one."

"For what, Ma?"

"For the good glasses." She meant the crystal wineglasses with the gold rims that had been passed down from Granny Webb and had stood inverted in the china cupboard for as long as he could remember. He had never known them to be used. Inside the china cupboard next to the glasses was a photograph of his father's mother in a black silk twill dress, looking freeze-dried and mournful.

"Where is that stupid mailman?" his mother said, pulling back the curtain and looking for the plume of dust along the road.

It was days before he had a chance to listen to the CD. It was on the way to the bank. The sounds of leaf susurration, cicadas, crickets, mortars, a calling bird with a voice like a kid hooting down a cardboard tube, snatches of talk, incoming fire, deafening helicopter fibrillation filled the truck. He was fascinated, listened to it again. And again.

Saturday was grocery day, but his mother said, "I don't feel up to it. You just get what we need, bread and eggs. Coffee. Whatever else you see that looks good. I don't have much appetite these days anyhow. And I want a wait for the mail. I'm expectin mail."

He bought the groceries and on the way out of town passed the library. Two miles beyond it he thought of books—books on Vietnam—and he turned around. He came away with three, all they had, read them in bed that night and fell asleep with a book on his face. He awoke frightened and shouting, thinking something was smothering him. The exhaled moisture from his mouth had formed a round dimple in the page.

It was not long after this that his mother began to give way. She would look at him and say, "Where's Gilbert? Out playin, I bet. I want him to fill up that wood box." And later she would tell him, "You'll have to fend for yourself for supper. I can't cook without no wood." He felt a pang of guilt for there had been many times when he was a boy that he had dodged the wood box. But she kept asking if the mail had come until Gilbert, exasperated, said, "You expectin a letter from the president or what?" She shook her head and said nothing.

In the year before the millennium, Gilbert's son Monty, a big dark-haired fellow, still single, who worked as a roofer in Colorado, turned thirty-two. Gilbert hadn't seen him in years. Rod, the younger one, lived in Sheridan a block away from his mother, worked in Buffalo in a video rental store. He was married and had two children, twin girls, whom Gilbert had only once seen and never had touched nor held. The little girls had never been to the ranch. The boy's wife, Debra, worked too, answering the telephone at Equality Cowboy Travel. Gilbert sometimes dreamed that they would have more children—sons—and that these little grandsons would love the ranch, would grow up knowing what a beautiful place the Wolfscales owned. They would love it as he did and take it on when he went.

Gilbert's mother, though tottery and crotchety, was eighty-one with no sign of giving up. The purple sponge, though somewhat faded, was largely unchanged, not to be used. She took to rummaging through the desk looking for pencil and paper, settled on a little notebook spiral-bound at the top and with lined paper. She spent hours at the kitchen table bent over this notebook, thinking, occasionally scrawling something down or erasing everything, tearing out the spoiled sheet and crumpling it.

"What are you writin, Ma? Your biography? Cowgirl poetry?"

"No," she said and put her arm around the notebook so he couldn't see it, like a child protecting a test paper from a cheating neighbor.

On a very cold March day he went into town to the ranch equipment center; the used aircraft tires he'd ordered for the bush hog were in. If the weather warmed up later in the week he'd work on pulling old sagebrush out of the three-mile pasture. In town the bank thermometer read –2 and a harsh wind made it seem like the freezing pits of hell. He ordered a pizza. Clouds were moving in as he drove back eating the cheesy slices, and as he turned into the ranch drive the first fine flakes drove through the air.

The house was silent. He thought his mother might be napping and went out to the shop, where he worked on changing the bush hog's tires. The days were growing longer, and he worked until twilight. Back in the house he was disturbed by the deep silence. Usually his mother watched crime programs on television at this hour. He went to her room and knocked on the door.

"Ma! Ma, you O.K.? I'm goin a start supper now." There was no answer. He opened the door and saw his mother would not again want any supper.

It was a shock to learn that her bank account was at flat zero. He couldn't understand what she had spent the money on. He remembered her telling him when she had broken her hip that she had over six thousand dollars set aside for "—*you* know." And he did know. For her funeral costs. He'd had to scratch to come up with the money for a decent coffin.

Cleaning out her room, he came across the spiral-bound notebook. It was filled with plaintive letters to the California State Allocation Department, asking when her inheritance would come. Folded in the front of the notebook was the original letter. He telephoned the number at the bottom of the page but got a message that the number had been disconnected. Gilbert began to guess there was some sort of scam. He called Sheriff Brant Smich, asked him if he knew anything about California State Allocation.

"Hell, yes. You get a letter from them sayin about you inherited some money and askin for your bank account numbers? Don't believe none of it. Don't answer them. Bring the letter to the post office. They're after that outfit for mail fraud."

With his mother gone, civilization began to fall away from him as feathers from a molting hen. In a matter of weeks he was eating straight from the frying pan.

As is usual in the ranch world, things went from bad to worse. The drought settled deeper, like a lamprey eel sucking at the region's vitals. He had half-seen the scores of trucks emblazoned CPC speeding along the dusty road for the last year, and knew that they were drilling for coal bed methane on BLM land adjacent to his ranch. They pumped the saline wastewater laden with mineral toxins into huge containment pits. The water was no good, he knew that, and it seemed a terrible irony that in such arid country water could be worthless. He had always voted Republican and supported energy development as the best way to make jobs in the rural hinterlands. But when the poison wastewater seeped from the containment pits into the ground water, into Bull Jump Creek, into his alfalfa irrigation ditches, even into the household well water, he saw it was killing the ranch.

He fought back. Like other ranchers who once again felt betrayed by state and federal government, he wrote letters and went to meetings protesting coal bed methane drilling, protesting the hundreds of service roads and drill rigs and heavy trucks that were tearing up the country. The meetings were strange, for ecological conservationists and crusty ranchers came together in the same room, in agreement for once. He noted with satisfaction that the schoolteacher, Dan Moorhen, a bleeding heart liberal ecology-minded freak, admitted that ranchers were the best defense against developers chopping up the land, that ranches and ranchers kept the old west alive. When the gas company reps or politicians came, the meetings were rancorous and loud, and at the end people signed petitions with such force their pens ripped the paper, but it all meant nothing. The drilling continued, the poison water seeped, the grass and sage and alfalfa on his land died. All he could do was hang on to the place.

He was unprepared for the telephone call from a neighbor, Fran Bangharmer. It was the morning of the Fourth of July.

"Too bad about Suzzy, all that right on the front page, too."

"What do you mean?" he said. "What was on the front page?"

"Arrested for embezzlin. Monday's paper."

"What!" He barely listened to her subtly triumphant voice, tinged with schadenfreude, but hung up as soon as he could and drove into town to find a three-day-old paper and read for himself that his ex-wife had, for years, been siphoning tax money into a private bank account by a complex series of computer sleights of hand he could not understand.

He went to the county jail and tried to see her but was turned away.

"She don't want to see you, Gib, and she's got that right."

Half of the stores in town were closed for the holiday. Already there were clusters of people along the sidewalk although the parade didn't start until one o'clock. In despair he drove down to Buffalo to the video store where Rod worked. It was open, the windows draped in red, white, and blue ribbons. A huge poster read:

RODEO DAYS! JULY 4 TO 10!

He found his younger son stocking the shelves with gaudy boxes. Standing behind him the father noticed the son's thinning hair and felt the hot breath of passing time.

"Rod?" he said, and the young man turned around.

"Dad." They looked at each other, and the son dropped his eyes. Gilbert could smell his son's aftershave lotion. He had never used the stuff in his life.

"I came to—I want to—well. Your mother?"

"Yeah. Do you want a have lunch?"

"You mean dinner?"

The son flushed at the old-fashioned word. "Yeah. 'Dinner.' Go down the KFC and eat in the car."

"I come in the truck. Come on, let's go."

"I got a tell somebody I'm goin."

That's what it was like, thought Gilbert, working for somebody else. You had to tell them whatever you did or were going to do and they could say no.

He drove to the fast food strip at the north end of town, shouted into the drive-through order box intercom. Sitting in the truck, the windows down and the hot sun burning their arms, they gnawed at the salty, overspiced chicken, huge crumbs falling. They both sucked on straws in vanilla milk shakes.

"I tried a see her," said Gilbert. "She wouldn't see me."

"She's still pretty bitter, you know. Feels like her life was wasted, or at least some years of it. She's that way. She takes a position and that's it. You can't argue her out of nothin. She's stubborn."

"I know that pretty well. How's it affectin *you* that your mother is a crook and a jailbird?" He glanced sideways at Rod, seeing the pale, indoor complexion, the dark, thick hair, clerk's shirt with creases ironed into the sleeves. The boy had the heavy Wolfscale jaw and beaky nose.

"Hell, I don't know. I don't think of it that way. People look at me kind a funny but they don't say nothin. Except Deb. She is gettin a lot a snide comment down at the travel agency. It's no fun for her. It's my girls I worry about, if some kid at school this fall is goin a taunt them. You know, 'Your granny stole money . . .'"

"Kids got short memories. By the time school starts they won't recall it. What do you think they'll do to her?"

"Probly go pretty light. She's got a good lawyer. You know she made restitution of about twelve grand. That'll count for a lot. They already got a lien on the house, repossessed her car. That's what she used the most a the money for, buy the house and fix it up. That house was everthing to her. She put in a swimmin pool two years ago."

"I used a wonder how she could afford it. I doubted clerks make that much money. And I heard a couple years ago that she went out to Las Vegas?" He couldn't believe he'd found a packet of salt beneath the flabby biscuit. Did anyone ever think their chicken not salty enough?

"It was a whole bunch a them that work at the county offices. They all went. She won four thousand bucks."

For some reason this remark incensed Gilbert. Rod said it in a tone of pride that his lying, cheating, stealing, double-dealing mother won some money gambling. He changed the subject abruptly. "What do you hear from your brother?"

"Aw, he calls up now and then. We get together with him when we take Arlene down to Denver for her treatment. You know she's had that cancer. It's in remission now and you'd never know she'd been sick a day."

Gilbert did not know she'd been sick a day. He shuddered. In the distance he could hear the high school marching band. The parade was starting early, or maybe just warming up.

"Is he still workin for that roofin contractor?"

"Well, no. He's workin in a restaurant. He's workin in a Jap restaurant. But he's healthy enough, thank God, considerin his—lifestyle."

"What does that mean, 'his lifestyle'?" Gilbert wiped his hands of the chicken, wadded the flimsy napkin, and thrust it into the grease-stained box.

"Well, he's—you know."

"I know what?"

"Dad, it's not up to me to say nothin about Monty." Rod was

folding and crushing the chicken box. He wiped his right hand on his pants leg.

"I ain't heard or seen him for quite a few years. Not likely to. Now what the hell is this about 'his lifestyle'?"

"For Christ sake, Dad. It's nothin. Just he's sort a—more—sophisticated. He likes a different kind a stuff than most people come from Wyomin."

"I hear you talkin but I don't know what you're sayin."

But he did. As a child Monty had hung around the kitchen and his mother constantly, and getting him to help with chores had been more labor than doing the jobs himself. That is until Myrl Otter came to work on the ranch on weekends. Myrl was a big blond Scandinavian type, muscular and good-looking. The man's wife had her work cut out for her keeping an eye on him as girls flirted with Myrl and he reciprocated willingly. After he came to work on the ranch Monty began to tag after the fellow like a yellowjacket after pears. Gilbert noticed, but as the boy was only seven or eight, it seemed just a little kid's fancy, nothing much. Kids got attached to dogs and blankets and maybe even hired men. He thought nothing of it, and within a few months Myrl Otter, in the way of so many ranch hands, didn't show up for work and Gilbert forgot him until now. The marching music, carried by the light wind, seemed nearer.

"I better get goin. Don't want a get tied up in that damn parade." He got out, threw his chicken box at the trash can. Rod, too, tossed his crumpled box, but it hit the side of the can and sprayed chicken bones.

"Forget it," said Gilbert. "They get paid a pick up."

He dropped Rod back at the video store and headed north, thinking to beat the parade by taking a side street, but he was too late. He stopped for a red light that wouldn't change and the parade came surging around a corner, passing in front of him, and he had to wait. A section of the high school band straggled past, sweaty kids, many of them obese, their white marching trousers bunched in the crotch. He remembered schoolmates in his own childhood, skinny quick ranch kids, no one fat and sweaty, Pete Kitchen looking like he was made of kindling wood and some insulation wire, Willis McNitt small enough to shit behind a sagebrush and never be noticed.

Behind the band came two teenage boys dressed as Indians, breechclouts over swim trunks, a load of beads around their necks, black wigs with braids and feathers. One carried a bongo drum, striking it irregularly with his hand. Their skins had been darkened with some streaky substance. Then two men whom he recognized as Sheridan car mechanics slouched along in buckskin suits and fur hats, carrying antique flintlocks. One had a demi-john, which he lifted to his lips every thirty seconds, crying "Yee-haw!" and the other had a few shiny No. 2 traps over his shoulder. Gilbert could see the hardware store price tags on them. Gilbert despaired. He knew he was going to get the whole hokey Wild West treatment before he could move.

Now came two horses, both bearing kids dressed as cowboys, heavy woolly chaps, pearl-button western shirts, limp bandannas, big hats, and boots. Both twirled guns on their fingers, aiming at friends in the crowd. They were followed by a stock outlaw and a sheriff's posse, and behind them half the town's women and small children in pioneer regalia—long dresses of calico, aprons and sunbonnets, big Nikes flashing incongruously with every step. One of these women was Patty Codenhead, and for a moment he was startled at how much she looked like his father's mother's photograph in the china cupboard. It was the costume, he thought. The parade came down to a few trick riders in neon satin, and Sedley Alwen, who crazy or not, was in every public procession showing his roping skills, stepping in and out of his fluid loops and somehow avoiding the horse manure that marked the path. The last of all was a CPC pickup, three hard-hatted methane gas workers sitting in back smoking cigarettes and joking with one another. Now he could go.

He could go, but he found it difficult to step on the accelerator. The light turned green, red, and green again, yet he couldn't move until drivers behind him began to sound their horns. There had been something wrong with the parade, something seriously wrong, but he couldn't think what.

Driving through the open country on the way back he forgot the parade and thought about Monty and what form his "sophistication" might take, about his embezzling wife, the other son who had not bothered to tell him that his youngest grandchild had cancer. He couldn't tell the size of things. He was very thirsty and blamed the salty chicken.

The buildings and traffic fell away and he was on the empty road, the dusty sage flying past, the white ground. The sky was a hard cheerful blue, empty but for a few torn contrails. Plastic bags impaled on the barb fences flapped in the hot wind. A small herd of antelope in the distance had their heads down. He saw his neighbor's cattle spread out on the parched land, and it came to him that there had been no ranchers in the parade—it was all pioneers, outlaws, Indians, and gas.

He knew what kind of furniture Jesus would pick for his place in Wyoming. He would choose a few small pines in the National Forest, go there at night, fell and limb them, debark the sappy rind with a spud, exposing the pale, worm-tunneled wood, and from the timbers he would make the simplest round-legged furniture, everything pegged, no nails nor screws.

He wished his mother was still alive. He'd say to her, "One thing sure. He wouldn't get hisself tangled up with no ranch." It didn't come close to saying what he meant, but it was all he could do.

The Old Badger Game

THIS HAPPENED LAST YEAR EAST OF THE POWDER RIVER country, somewhere in the Wyoming breaks. It's not much of a story, the kind of thing you might hear on a sluggish afternoon in Pee Wee's.

Three old bachelor badgers lived a certain distance from one another on a piece of rough ground in the back pasture of Frank Frink's ranch. The badgers were concerned with food, sunbathing, and property lines. Their territories came together in a stony outcrop that faced south and where the scenery flung out like an opened fan. Here, in the morning sunshine, the three badgers met, exchanged remarks on the vagaries of life and recent wind speeds in the whistles, grunts, and growls that pass for communication among them. One of the badgers had held down a teaching job at the university up in Bozeman for a few years— creative writing or barge navigation—but had retired to the ranch. Two of the trio, including the university badger, were stout and ordinary. The third had a reddish tinge to his fur but was as ignorant as a horseshoe.

The Frink ranch started a hundred and fourteen years ago with some Texas longhorns and a restless pair of cowboys blackballed out of the Lone Star State for their sympathies with the LS cowboy strike of 1883. Since then the place had rolled through a dozen sets of hands until it came to Frink.

Frank Frink took an interest in immortality and fountains of youth, eternal flames and the like, and because he had persuaded himself that he was going to live, if not forever, at least to be two hundred, he was conservation-minded and absolute death on overgrazing. He was constantly shifting his cattle to different pastures and had an immense and complex chart on the pantry door that showed the schedule of short-term grazing he had worked out. One delicate pasture with live water held cattle for no more than three hours before they were hustled off to coarser grass.

Frink was always shorthanded. You ranchers know how hard it is to get good help. He found it just as hard to get bad help as he skimped on pay in favor of saving up for his long twilight years. At roundup time he was shorthanded and begged his wife to help drive.

"Oh all right," she said, "but I'm telling you right now that I need a new winter coat and after we ship the cattle I better get it."

"Haaah," said Frink, who had heard of the coat before.

On the circle drive the rancher's wife came out of a draw, and as she trotted past a saltbush a badger appeared.

"Good-looking badger," she said aloud, imagining herself in a coat of the same red hue, not necessarily a fur coat—faux fur would do, or even tweed with a monkey-fur collar.

Toward dawn the three badgers congregated at the stony outcrop.

"Have a good hunt?" asked one of the ordinary badgers.

"Not bad," said the other. "You?"

"Fair. How about you, Red?"

"Well, Great Badger Almighty, the rancher's wife has fell in love with me. I suppose she'll be pesterin me all the time now."

"What? What are you sayin?"

"Aw, she seen me over in the saltbush draw, says, 'That's the handsomest badger I ever seen, I'm crazy about him.'"

The other badgers laughed and made coarse jokes about possible and impossible sexual conjunctions between the red-haired badger and the rancher's wife. Inevitably the talk turned to the story that went back to the 1880s of a desperate cowboy who forced himself on an ill-tempered grandmother badger and the violent consequences, which still tickled a low sense of humor.

"I haven't got time to lay around," said Red, and he ambled away, taking a route through a deep draw where a number of noxious exotics, including a monstrous teasel plant, grew. He dragged himself through the teasel bush until his fur was sleek and shining.

"She should see me now," he said to the teasel.

Frank Frink and two of his cronies came out of the kitchen door, their hands full of ginger cookies shaped like steer heads with frosting eyes. The rancher stopped dead.

"Look at that. There it is again."

"What?" said Crisp Braid, scanning near and far, seeing nothing unusual.

"In the ditch. The biggest goddamn badger I have yet saw. Make a rug half as big as a steer hide. This is about the tenth time I've sawn the bastard. Havin coffee the other mornin and I look out the window over the sink, there's this bugger layin on a rock all spraddled out takin its ease and airin its balls like it was in a hammock. I went for the .30-06, took a shot, and missed. Know what he done? Kicked dirt at me. Damn these cookies or I'd run get the 06 now." He ate two steer heads at once and choked a little, the sound enough to send the badger into the weeds.

*   *   *

"How's that love affair, Red?" asked one of the dull badgers a few weeks later. "Got her down yet?"

"No. Rancher caught on and he's crazy jealous. Can't get near her he's jumpin up after a gun."

The university badger remarked that that was how the old badger game went—what seemed imminent somehow never came to pass. Life, in short, was a shuck. But then, he'd been denied tenure and was a little sour on things.

Man Crawling Out of Trees

Mᴵᵀᶜᴴᴱᴸᴸ Fᴀɪʀ ᴀɴᴅ ʜɪs ᴡɪꜰᴇ, Eᴜɢᴇɴɪᴇ, sᴘᴇᴅ ᴏᴠᴇʀ ᴛʜᴇ whiskey-colored plains in their aging Infiniti, "cutting prairie," said Mitchell under his breath, thinking it sounded western. In an hour they had covered the same ground that would have taken the old oxcart emigrants, trailing a wake of graves, almost a week. It was September, and they were on their way back to Wyoming after a visit to Maine, where their daughter, Honor, lived with her boyfriend and a new baby boy. The road was wet from a thunderstorm, and under the late afternoon sun the asphalt gleamed as though drenched with oil. The indigo cloud from which the rain had fallen packed the sky behind them, and on the hood of the car the wind scrolled beads of water into strings of minuscule droplets, like the dotted lines cartoonists use to indicate trumpet blasts.

It had been a shock to Mitchell, after several years in Wyoming, to see New England again—its maddening choked roads, tangled brush, the trees absorbing light, all drenched in shadow. The tepid air, unmoved by wind, seemed stifling. The house in which their daughter lived was a log heap built sometime in the 1930s, a copy of an Adirondack lodge but with decaying sills and warped doors. It perched at the edge of a lake rich with algae, and was the property of their daughter's boyfriend's aunt, who called it a "cottage." The lake gave off a gassy smell. They approached the house on an uneven flagstone walk through tall and uncut grass. The neighboring cottages, which huddled around the shoreline like wet hens, showed garish plastic toys in their yards, and Eugenie guessed these were summer rentals. While they stayed in the house Eugenie sneezed with the regularity of a perpetual motion machine, plagued by her old allergy to molds.

Honor and Chaz called their baby Hal, a mercy, for they had named him Halyard, the namesake, said Mitchell in a disgusted voice, of a rope on a sailboat.

"Why would they do that?" he asked that night as they lay in the dank twin beds.

Eugenie said nothing, but she knew the importance of giving a baby a distinctive name, whether for a rope, a French novelist, or even an empress.

Their daughter's boyfriend, Chaz, was as old as Mitchell, his hair well in retreat and accentuated by a compensatory ponytail. He was vaguely handsome and evasive with questions on the nature of his income, muttering something about consulting work. He made light conversation about golf with Mitchell, and to Eugenie he chattered about restaurants and wine.

Honor worked three afternoons a week as a dispatcher for Pine Tree Security, a roster of retired urban policemen patrolling millionaires' second homes on the pond, imitating shivering loon calls as they drove, in practice for an annual contest. The contest began in 1987 after the last pair of real loons on the lake disappeared. Eugenie tried to worm Chaz's occupational information out of Honor, who turned silent and then said meanly, "I'll tell you about Chaz when you tell me who my real father is." After that remark Eugenie went out on the porch to light a cigarette and shoot streams of smoke into the hazy air. She rarely smoked and had to ask Honor for the cigarette—awkward in the extreme.

At the end of the week Eugenie told her daughter she should come out to Wyoming for a visit, bring the baby.

"We *will* talk." It was her way of making peace. She didn't mention Chaz. Honor smiled a little, lightly touched her mother's hand. But beneath the tranquil moment throbbed their shared knowledge, as discordant as when a pause comes during a piano sonata and the raucous monotone of a nearby radio rapper seeps in like blood in water.

The next day Mitchell and Eugenie left for Wyoming. At the car Honor spun and suddenly kissed Mitchell goodbye full on the mouth, an undaughterly kiss from which Mitchell broke away in confusion.

"Now where did she find *him*," said Mitchell, wiping at his lips as though to remove the raw flavor of his daughter's mouth as they crept along the narrow road. The sullen sky sagged lower and it began to rain. This landscape was no longer big enough for him. The long sight lines and rearing mountains of Wyoming had got into his bones.

"Oh God," said Eugenie. "Poor Honor. Those dark circles. She just doesn't get any rest, taking care of the baby and working too."

"Like to know what *he* does. Nothing, I bet. He's got that look. Probably lived off women all his life. She'll dump him, I hope. God, these lousy roads." A front tire thumped into a pothole, and ahead of them, as far as the eye could see, was a wavering parade of more holes gleaming with rainwater. A logging truck passed them, and beneath its weighted wheels Mitchell could almost see the ragged asphalt crumbling. The Infiniti seemed to crawl through the gloom.

"He's sort of the kind of guy you meet in line at the deli," said Eugenie, "and you both say how good the imported olives are." She was glad the visit was over, relieved to be away from her daughter's accusing eye. Honor had held the grudge for more than three years, thanks to bigmouthed Dr. Playfire. It seemed she wasn't going to get over it.

They emerged from New England's lowering trees and over-loaded roads and several days later reached the end of endless Nebraska, crossed the Wyoming border. Mitchell, who had been irritable on the whole trip, brightened despite the scruffy dandruff of billboards and signs that marred the approach to Cheyenne. A quarter of a mile to their right a cattle train labored. Eugenie punched the CD tracks back to her favorite, Jimmie Dale Gilmore singing nasally about Dallas and a DC-9. Mitchell, who pre-ferred classical music, tried to remember what a DC-9 had looked like, could only come up with a hazy recollection of a short, fat plane with propellers, of scratchy seats and a dismal bus-station smell. He doubted there was still a DC-9 in operation anywhere on the continent. Well, maybe in Canada. And Jimmie Dale Gilmore, or whoever had written the song, must now be embar-rassed that he had ever been awed by either a DC-9 or Dallas.

The train tracks veered south, and the train swung away from the highway, taking the cows to slaughterhouses. They could see the dark bodies through the perforated metal sides of the cars. Eugenie waved at the disappearing train. Mitchell glanced at her. As she had aged, the classic profile had thickened, the delicate cheeks became slabs of rouged flesh, the chin lost its clean line, and her nose coarsened. At the sides of her mouth were tiny curved lines like the bends in fishhooks. But the black hair was the same, a few tendrils curling in front of her ears like inked draw-ings of a scrolled fiddle neck, and to strangers she presented the dramatic look of a woman with a story.

A semi, tyrannosaurus of the interstate, passed them, swaying. "Doing ninety anyway," he said. "I'm right on seventy-five." Mitchell hated semis and usually Eugenie made a noise in her throat to indicate that she, too, disliked the big trucks, a pretense that arose from the deeper pretense of wifely subordination to a husband's opinions. This time she didn't answer, thumbing through the CDs in the zippered carrying case. There was nothing she wanted to hear, hadn't heard over and over on the way east. They should have bought some books on tape. At least she hadn't had to listen to Mitchell's lugubrious quartets and motets and symphonies. Before they left Wyoming she had caught him going through his precious CD collection.

"Don't bring that stuff," she said flatly. Now she switched the console to radio and caught *Car Talk*. Both brothers were laughing hysterically and a third laugher was adding to the din. Mitchell pointed to a multicolored herd of horses beyond a fence.

"How did it go again? Come on, Bawb, make the sound your car made. . . ."

An incredible series of wheezes, gurgles, snorts, and panting sounds issued from the radio, accompanied by soaring laughter. Eugenie laughed with the whooping brothers.

"Shut it off, will you?"

"I thought you liked *Car Talk*. It's about cars."

"I *know* it's about cars. Maybe ten percent of it. The rest is hyena howling and asking women how they spell their names."

In the silence that followed he became aware of a faint wheezing sound from the Infiniti. As he listened he heard other abnormal sounds. Everything suddenly began to rattle and shimmy. In the backseat the box containing truffled walnut oil, jars of French cornichons, juniper berries, the tins of Eugenie's favorite *macarons de Saint-Jean-de-Luz,* and a few bottles of Graham's 2000 vintage port, all things they could not find in Wyoming, clinked and knocked. He stretched out his arm and turned the radio back on.

"How do you spell that, T-h-e-r-e-s-a or T-e-r-e-s-a . . ." Eugenie turned the radio off.

"What did you do that for?"

"I didn't want to hear them doing the name-spelling thing either."

The Infiniti was running smoothly again, and he remembered there was a rough patch somewhere along this stretch of highway—that must have been it.

A few miles beyond blustery Elk Mountain, Mitchell said, "Look at that."

"What?"

"The smoke that damn semi's making." He pointed his chin in the direction of the east-bound lane and she saw it a mile ahead, one of thousands of eighteen-wheeled trucks on the road, differing only in the billows of diesel smoke pouring from it. But as they drew abreast enormous orange flames shot into the air. The truck pulled over on the shoulder and they could see that a tarpaulin rolled up behind the cab was on fire. The driver jumped out and ran in front of his truck shouting into a cell phone.

"Hah!" said Mitchell with something like satisfaction. "It'll be an hour before anybody gets here."

The stench of smoke penetrated the Infiniti and they both thought of New York.

In midafternoon Mitchell turned north. It was five o'clock when they hit the familiar dirt road after the FIREWORKS sign. They crossed the tracks and the terrain began to rise, a little rumpled and showing bits of dark red ledge beyond the fences. A dozen pronghorn grazed a mile away and he slowed, watching the guard duty animal throw up its head suspiciously. As they drove a billow of dust rose behind them. It was a hopeless chore, trying to keep the car clean. A small stream, known locally as a river and faced with flattened junk cars to prevent erosion in the spring floods, threaded down from the rough foothills. They could see the dark ridge, the aspen grove that marked Star Lily Ranch in the distance. A mile beyond the cattle guard they crossed the railroad tracks again, the Infiniti thumping painfully. At the fork he bore right and the road climbed, took its most beautiful turn through the heart of dappling aspen, then opened out into a series of folded meadows.

Their house was in one of the meadows, sheltered to the southeast by a broad band of aspen which someone had told him were mysteriously dying. When he mentioned this to Eugenie she had said "Oh no," for she had a reverence for trees, the sycamore tree in Brooklyn, the beech and maple of Vermont, and here, where trees were lacking, she immediately elevated aspen to high rank.

In the aspen grove he had come upon the old wrought-iron sign that had once crowned the entrance to the ranch from which their lot had been sliced. It read simply PANAMA. The original owner of the place had worked in his youth on the Isthmus of Panama as an express shipment clerk for Wells Fargo. Now the metal arch lay facedown in the dirt. Mitchell dug it up, cleaned the leaf mold from it with a stick, and leaned it against an aspen. It was too heavy to carry. He would come one day with the truck and get it.

A mile farther on and they could see the dark mass of lodgepole pine and Engelmann spruce curved around their meadow like an encircling arm. The chimney was just visible, and Eugenie knew that the first thing Mitchell would do was light a fire in the fireplace, pour a drink, and sit in front of the fire, mesmerizing himself with the twisting flames while she defrosted two steaks. They were both on the diet that went for red meat and salad.

At the bottom of the hill they saw there had been a change in the village while they were gone.

"Look," said Eugenie. "It's the old woman. She's not dead and she's got a new house."

Mrs. Conkle's scabrous trailer was gone. In its place was a

small log cabin. The old woman was outside, smacking a stick at a sagebrush. She seemed made from sagebrush and rock herself.

Mitchell had met Eugenie Prower in the mid-1970s at Bennington College in Vermont and they had married in a round barn. The farmer who owned the barn had asked—and received—a thousand dollars in rental. Eugenie had then had the face of Pallas Athena, with a straight nose, a small chiseled mouth, and black hair pulled into a low knot at the nape of her neck. She was big-boned with a full bosom and comfortable hips. There was no indication that she would slowly change into a full-jawed Queen of Diamonds decked in ornate chokers and turtlenecked Peruvian sweaters. Back in those early days she told him she loved classical music, and only gradually did he realize that she meant some syrupy string ensemble that played popular medleys. It hadn't mattered because he thought she would learn to like the real music.

At the end of their barn wedding ceremony Mitchell had had a sudden and awful vision of his new wife, naked and down on all fours, looking beseechingly at the farmer, who was coming at her with a milking machine. As if Eugenie had read Mitchell's thought she fired a hard glance that struck him like a hurled shot glass. For her part, Eugenie saw him as a weird stranger, his narrow head and smooth Nordic features startlingly similar to a photograph she had seen of a preserved corpse pulled from a Scandinavian bog. There had been a braided leather rope around the ancient neck, the man choked in ritual death. She wanted to shout "No!" But in a few minutes they were running through the rice gauntlet, on their way to married life with no thoughts of milking machines or leathery bog men.

Through the childless years they had been tolerably content with each other, perhaps because early on they had bought an old farmhouse in Vermont, which served as a cooling-off retreat for one or the other when they quarreled. Mitchell was an architect with Dyer, Foxcap and Waigwa in Manhattan, and Eugenie one of several designers at her family's kitchen and bath design business, Prower and Baggs. Her mother had started the business in the 1950s designing country kitchens with gingham curtains, geraniums, and sunny breakfast nooks styled after some mythical Bucks County farmhouse. Now everything was sleek, grey, and German.

Their house in Brooklyn Heights was a brownstone whose feature was a sycamore at the back filling the summer space with luxurious rustling shade. In the winter Eugenie, who took a class at the Brooklyn Botanic Garden in ways to attract birds to the backyard, hung out feeders and kept a journal on the avian fauna that came to them. These were the years before the snake entered the garden.

Then Mitchell had an affair with an architectural graduate student intern. Eugenie did not confront him but waited it out, her emotions and thoughts a puree of insult and anger. When it was finished, she had a vengeful affair of her own with a handsome assistant cabinet liaison named Taylor. He was six years younger than she and the role of an experienced older woman initiating an innocent into the pleasures of love gratified her ego. They took long, long lunch hours, extending into late afternoon, to rush to "their" hotel, where Eugenie paid. But her affection for Taylor curdled overnight when, following the long Presidents' Day weekend, he told her he did not want to go on with the stolen meetings. He had gone to Mount Tremblant with friends and, as he put it, had met someone for whom he "cared very deeply."

"What, in forty-eight hours you developed this deep emotion?"

"Yes," he said stubbornly, his face flaming.

"Fine," she said. "Fine." But back at the office she had remarked privily to key people that she did not think Taylor was cut out for the kitchen and bath business, that he had poor design sense, that his three-hour lunches were meetings with Downtown Kitchens (DTK), to whom he was spilling his guts about the new suede-covered cabinets, that he was plotting to go over to DTK and God knew what clients he would try to take with him. But already it was too late; already the moment had arrived as when the woodman's arms reach the apogee of the swing and the ax begins its irrevocable descent, the moment at which, for the tree, everything changes. Eugenie was pregnant.

They had named the baby Honor because Eugenie had been moved by Honoré de Balzac's *Le Père Goriot* in her French class. Mitchell believed their daughter had been conceived in their five-legged bed, the supernumerary leg a wizened center-positioned stick with a metal glide foot. It was meant to give extra support but failed and beat counterpoint against the floor when they made love. Worse than the rapping leg was Eugenie's assortment of plans, blueprints, and new design books. She studied them for hours while Mitchell flopped and sighed ostentatiously, yanking pillows and covers over his head. In the morning they would both wake with the marks of books and bound plans on them. And the blueprints were often damaged, creased and torn.

One morning Mitchell fell asleep on the subway, transported back and forth for hours until groping fingers inside his jacket woke him. This happened, he said, because Eugenie's lamp and the crackling papers had kept him awake all night. That evening he made up a bed on the sofa and the next morning said he had not had such a good sleep in years. Eugenie too had enjoyed the extra space, shoved sketches and elevations onto Mitchell's side of the bed. It was a relief not to hear him mumbling in his sleep as he rowed through his gluey ocean of dreams.

Mitchell slept on the sofa for weeks until Eugenie noticed that the living room had absorbed his stale odor. That Saturday they flipped a coin for the spare room, more of a storage place than a guest room, and it had come up tails. Mitchell took their old bedroom and bought a new CD player for himself. Eugenie got the spare room, cleared out the boxes and plastic storage bins of winter clothes, repainted the walls a melon color, and spent a small fortune for dark blue tailored drapes that gave the space a slightly masculine flavor. There was a niche where she put the baby's cot. She put a luggage rack at the foot of the bed and on it a gilded Italian lacquer tray. In two days the tray was stacked with notebooks of ideas for dream kitchens glittering with copper in which no one would ever cook.

Eugenie and Honor sat together on a red leather sofa when Dr. Playfire said Honor could not be a kidney donor for Mitchell because neither her DNA nor her blood type matched. Eugenie felt the blood rise in her face, her heart thrummed with hatred for the pink-chopped doctor, whose eyes were bright with malice and who obviously relished the news he was breaking. She said nothing.

In the elevator Honor burst out. "My God! Who *is* my father?"

"Someone else, obviously," said Eugenie.

"But who? What happened? Were you married to someone else?"

"I don't intend to discuss it," said Eugenie in a glacier voice.

The elevator stopped and a man in a wheelchair pushed by a young woman got on. They rode in vibrating silence to the ground floor, Honor clenching her fists and glaring at her mother. In the car Eugenie held her silence while Honor wept, shouted, and demanded until she was hoarse and choking. Neither of them told Mitchell what Dr. Playfire had said—that Mitchell was not Honor's biological father—and Mitchell's youngest sister, Paula, became his kidney donor.

Honor left home while Mitchell was still in the hospital. New York changed and Eugenie was afraid and talked with Mitchell about getting out of the city. By then they could no longer go to the farmhouse in Vermont, for they had sold it in 1997. Mitchell, who had been thinking about Montana during his recuperation, read an article in *Personal Finance* that named Wyoming as a state with low property taxes and no income tax at all. It seemed a safe haven as well—an unlikely target as the state's entire population could fit into a phone booth. He recalled a childhood summer camp in the Tetons, singing around a campfire, fishing on Jenny Lake, and exploring Yellowstone trails on horseback.

Gradually Eugenie and Mitchell began to think Wyoming might be both an adventure and a sensible move. Mitchell, recovered from his kidney transplant, asked for semiretirement—he would fly from Wyoming to New York every two months, stay a few days. Eugenie said she could finally start on the two books she wanted to write: *The* Real *Urban Kitchen—Takeout & Deli* and *Global Kitchen*.

They made a trip out to scout around. Mitchell was stunned by the beauty of the place, not the overphotographed jags of the Grand Tetons but the high prairie and the luminous yellow distance, which pleased his sense of spatial arrangement. He felt as though he had stumbled into a landscape never before seen on the earth and at the same time that he had been transported to the *ur*-landscape before human beginnings. The mountains crouched at every horizon like dark sleeping animals, their backs whitened by snow. He trod on wildflowers, glistening quartz crystals, on agate and jade, brilliant lichens. The unfamiliar grasses vibrated with light, their incandescent stalks lighting the huge ground. Distance reduced a herd of cattle to a handful of tossed cloves. His heart squeezed in, and he wished for a celestial eraser to remove the fences, the crude houses, the one he bought included, from this place. Even the sinewy, braided currents of the wind, which made Eugenie irritable, pleased him.

Before they looked for a house they outfitted themselves at a Western Wear store, Eugenie buying two fringed suede skirts, some high-necked Cattle Kate blouses, and a pair of Rocket-buster boots featuring turquoise skeletons. Mitchell got into jeans, a western-cut shirt with pearl buttons. He bought a butter-colored pair of Olathe boots that slammed like a trip-hammer wherever he walked. He stumbled a lot, unable to get used to high heels, especially as he'd just got his first pair of bifocals. He bought a twenty-year-old pickup with four-wheel drive, dark green and dented, something he had always wanted, had a CD player installed, and took to driving around with his elbow out the window. He marveled at the truck's lack of rust.

"No salt on the roads here," he crowed.

Eugenie gave him a look as though he'd said he preferred his morning egg raw.

They stayed in Jackson while they looked for a house and property. Eugenie wanted to be near the Tetons, Yellowstone Park, and the national forests, but the cheapest places cost millions. Wyoming's easy taxes were almost negated by the extraordinarily high prices for property; scruffy sagebrush with bad water nine hundred feet down priced at breathtaking amounts if there was a mountain range in view. Mitchell began to think of these prop-erties as widows' windfalls. He imagined poor old ranchers work-ing themselves into early graves holding on to their places. And when they died the widows dumped the cows and called up the real estate brokers, who sketched out thirty-five-acre ranchettes. The widows then hightailed it to condos in Boca Raton—with the exception of Eleanora Figg.

*   *   *

The Fairs bought one of these ex-pasture plots thirty miles from Pinedale in a gated cluster of "estates" named Star Lily Ranch. They were three miles from the tiny town of Swift Fox, population seventy-three, fitted out with a general store and the Sagebrush Café. At dusk a globe of light like an incandescent jellyfish formed above Swift Fox and stained the mountainy darkness the weak orange of civilization.

The house stood on a sunny slope of wildflowers and silver sage with a view of the Bachelor range, which even in summer resembled a monstrous slab of halvah veined with mauve chocolate. In the distance the Wind Rivers lay against the horizon like crumpled envelopes.

The house, like every other house in Star Lily Ranch, was constructed of enormous pine logs. It was not the timber castle of some of their neighbors, but still, with 4,200 square feet, the largest house of their lives. The interior, designed in the grand *rancho* style of the 1980s, featured a gargantuan living room, intricate log notches, the distant mountains fitted artfully into the vast window, against which birds broke their heads.

Eugenie pronounced the kitchen a mess of cracked tile, greasy walls, tiny sink. She hated the elderly refrigerator's menacing snarl. Brown nylon carpet covered the living room and bedroom floors, the history of the former occupants written in its stains and chair-leg dents. The five bedrooms were tiny and dark. Eugenie set to work remaking the place with a loan from her mother.

"We'll take out these walls," she said, gesturing at the narrow dining room, the kitchen, the oversize living room. "We'll make a Great Room, so the space flows from the kitchen end to the dining space to the relaxation area."

"This one and that one are load-bearing walls," said Mitchell, squinting at the ceiling. "You can't take those out."

"We'll see. I'll get a builder in next week and go over the whole place with him. And those grim little bedrooms. If we knock out a couple of walls we'll have two good-size rooms. And put in some decent bay windows. There should be a terrific view of the mountains from the bedrooms."

The real estate agent, deeply tanned and wearing an expensive hat with a buckaroo telescope crease, had suggested that one of the bedrooms would make a nice home theater. Eugenie noticed that his tan had an orange cast, and beneath his strong cologne she detected the charred smell of chemical tanning lotion.

"You know," he said, "you're the first people from New York I ever sold a house to. We don't get New Yorkers here. Not their kind a place, I guess."

"My God," said Mitchell sotto voce to Eugenie, "all of this to look at"—he gestured at the tawny landscape, the distant mountains—"and he says 'home theater'?"

They both marveled at the astonishing wildlife, but for Eugenie the animals and birds were a decorative novelty. Mitchell, on the other hand, fell deeply in love with the pronghorn, those supreme athletes of the animal world which had evolved on the high plains over 20 million years along with wolves and bison. He called them "antelope." Their coloration—a reddish brown accented by sparkling white—reminded him of a pair of golf shoes he had once owned.

Eugenie found Mitchell in the attic one day rummaging through the boxes they had never unpacked—city clothes, old financial records that might be needed someday, a miscellany of odds and ends.

"What *are* you looking for?"

"My old golf shoes," he said, straightening up under the purlins.

"Golf shoes! Mitchell, you told me to get rid of all your golf stuff back when you had the transplant."

"Yes," he said, "but I thought the shoes might have made it."

"Well, they didn't. Why do you want them, anyway? I can't believe you are thinking of taking up golf again."

"No." He couldn't say that it was because he had wanted to see how closely the golf shoes had resembled pronghorn. That first winter he mourned when he read in the local paper that in a snowstorm a semi had plowed into a small herd of pronghorn on I-80 and killed seventeen animals.

Wyoming had seemed civilized when they first moved out, but gradually evidence appeared that forced them to recognize that they were in a place people in the east would regard as peripheral to the real world. There were disturbing proofs that the weight of a harsh past still bore down with force. Every few months something inexplicably rural happened: on a back road one man shot another with his great-grandfather's 45.70 vintage buffalo gun; a newcomer from Iowa set out for an afternoon hike, and fell off a cliff as she descended Wringer Mountain. Black bears came down in September and smashed Eugenie's bird feeders. A hawk hid under the potentilla bush and leaped suddenly on an overconfident prairie dog a little too far from its burrow. In Antler Spring, the town where they bought their liquor and groceries, a young woman expecting her first child was widowed when her husband, fighting summer wildfires in Colorado, was killed by a Pulaski tool that fell from a helicopter. Vacationers locked themselves out of their cars and were struck by lightning. Ranchers, their eyes on their cattle, drove off the road and overturned. Everything seemed to end in blood.

Outside the Star Lily Ranch community Eleanora Figg was their nearest neighbor. She was an elderly widow rancher in her mid-seventies of the classic Republican, conservative, art-hating, right-wing, outspoken, flint-faced type. She ran both cattle and some sheep, drove an ancient black Jeep. She loathed environmentalists and people from somewhere else. Mitchell understood the bumper sticker on her Jeep—SHOOT, SHOVEL AND SHUT UP—to express her opinions on wolves. She had taken one look at the Fairs' Infiniti and recognized them as sybarites who dined on camel heels and foreign olives. She herself lived on home-killed beef, boiled potatoes, and black coffee. She was always dressed in jeans, manure-caked boots, and a ragged barn coat. When they first met, Mitchell shook the old woman's hand, feeling the coarse, hard fingers gripping his own with remarkable strength.

"How's your teeth?" she said. "Pretty sharp?"

"I don't know," said Mitchell, nonplussed by the odd question. "Why?"

"Always lookin for somebody help us castrate lambs."

At the post office the woman told him about Eleanora Figg.

"Her and her boys Condor and Tommy just about run this place." She added that there had been a third son, Cody, who had died of heatstroke hiking in the Grand Canyon on his first and only vacation.

He had met Condor Figg. The first winter he learned the hard way that the truck he had bought was best as a summer truck. It skidded and slewed in the lightest snow. The inevitable happened, and while he was trying to call a tow truck on his cell phone, damning the hundreds of Wyoming dead spots that made smoke signals more practical than cell phones, a big flatbed truck carrying a thousand-pound roll of hay pulled up.

"Got a chain?" yelled the driver, a big chunky man wearing a T-shirt despite the cold and snow. He had a curly black beard and eyes as narrow and darting as two fingerling trout.

"No," said Mitchell, and before his mouth closed the man was out of the truck and dragging a heavy chain with hook ends from it. In less than forty seconds he had the chain wrapped around

Mitchell's trailer hitch and the truck up on the road, pointed the wrong way.

"My God," said Mitchell, "how can I thank you?" He fumbled for money, looking at the hole in the snow where the truck had been. Beyond the fence thirty or forty pronghorn grazed with cool detachment. He rushed on, his voice fast out of his throat. "My name's Mitchell Fair. We live in Star Lily Ranch." And he held out a twenty-dollar bill.

The man looked at him with hatred. "Yeah. I know. Keep your money. Where your house sets is where my folks had a stock tank. When old Dean Peraine had that truck you bought off a him he run it ever weather for damn near ten years. Had some weight to her. Never went off the road unless he wanted to." He jumped in the big truck, stood on the gas, and was gone in a blast of blue smoke. But Mitchell put four hundred pounds of sand-bags in the bed of his truck and his winter driving skills improved. He stayed on the road.

There was another old woman in Swift Fox—Mrs. Conkle. She was also a rancher's widow but lived in a decrepit trailer with a yellow stucco exterior. Over the years wind-driven dirt had discolored the structure as the stucco cracked and buckled into a leprous mass. Sometimes when the Fairs drove past they saw the old woman outside, struggling to hang some wet grey garments on a drooping clothesline.

"That old thing," said Eugenie. "You have to wonder how somebody gets to that state."

Mitchell, who talked with local people more than she did, had heard a tale of hard luck and swindle.

The day the Fairs left Swift Fox on their journey to Maine they had passed Mrs. Conkle's ugly trailer. The yard was full of trucks, and men were coming from the trailer carrying a bureau, a box of canning jars, a rocking chair.

"Ah," said Eugenie. "There must have been a fire. Or maybe

the poor old lady died and the relatives are going through her things."

Mitchell didn't think so. As they neared the bottom of the hill, coming toward them was Condor Figg's flatbed loaded with lumber and logs. In the side mirror Mitchell saw him turn in to Mrs. Conkle's yard.

Mitchell was glad to be back in Wyoming, far from Maine, and in a way Eugenie was not displeased though the place seemed as alien as ever. The air was clear and the sunlight so fierce that the subtle colors of lichen and rock, of dusty sage leaf burned with an intensity the clouded east could never know. A few days after their return the first storm flailed a few yellow leaves from the aspen and beat down the summer grasses. Weeds collapsed under the hard frost that followed. Then came ten days of flawless clarity, radiantly golden days in the shimmering aspen groves. From the lodgepole pine on the slopes above twisted ribbons of resinous scent.

"It *is* beautiful," Eugenie agreed. She walked out on the forest trail near the house several times where the odor was of dry duff, of earth scratched about by bears raiding squirrel hoards. Her walks stopped abruptly when she met a hunter. He looked wretched and tough, bowlegged, his face smeared with blacking, a trickle of blood in front of his ear where a branch had pierced the skin. He carried a powerful-looking bow, and the razor points of his arrows glittered. He glared at her with his wolfish eyes. She could smell a sharp odor.

"You ought a be wearin orange. Get yourself shot in that getup."

She was wearing her brown suede jacket and suddenly realized that from a distance, to someone peering through the trees, she might briefly resemble a deer. Perhaps this man had even trained an arrow on her. She could not speak. She turned and began walking rapidly toward the trailhead. At a bend in the trail she turned around and was frightened to see him following. She ran then for the parking lot, expecting to feel an arrow in her back or a hand clamped over her mouth. She said nothing to Mitchell because he had remarked several times that it was hunting season and they ought to get orange vests.

In late October the first snowstorms arrived and steady cold began building the drifts. A few deer came to Eugenie's bird feeders and she put out pie pans of sunflower seed for them. In less than a week there was a herd of fifty mule deer in their yard at dusk and Eugenie thought of the bow hunter and was glad the deer were safe from him. The wind blew the pie pans away, and she got Mitchell to pour the contents of the twenty-pound bags directly on the ground near a clump of rabbitbrush. The deer ate all of the seed each night, and soon they were spending seventy dollars a week on sunflower seed. Foxes also came for the seed, and magpies, Steller's jays, even a northern flicker, which seemed the wrong kind of bird to patronize a feeder. Mitchell said he should buy a rifle as one deer would be a good investment on their birdseed expenses.

"God," said Eugenie disgustedly.

"You will never see anything like this back east," she wrote to Honor. "Fantastic wildlife, although Mitchell now wants to start killing it." She was careful not to write "your father." The daughter, who never wrote letters, telephoned and said she had moved out of the cottage and into an apartment in Brooklyn, that Hal was cutting teeth and was awful with crying and fussing, that he was at day care because Honor had found a wonderful job with a group that made socially responsible documentary films for television.

"Still, it's not easy," she said.

"Do you need some money?" asked Eugenie. She was so glad

to talk to Honor she nearly cried. Until that moment she had not realized how miserable she was in Wyoming with only Mitchell. She knew people talked about them. When she went into the Swift Fox store for eggs silence fell. If she remarked that it was a beautiful day there was a pause, then some hearty voice said it sure was and the silence came again. As she shut the door behind her she could hear the sudden babble of voices inside. The woman at the post office, herself an outsider, said, "Oh, they'll accept you up to the fence, but they'll never let you open the gate."

"Money?" said Honor. "Well, I could use it. Rent day seems to come around pretty fast. The job doesn't pay much, but there's a good chance that it will if I can stick with it." Her voice sounded cheery and confident, and Eugenie suddenly missed her own old job and smart, good New York talk, missed noon-hour shopping and being able to find anything she needed or wanted, missed the restaurants and the museums. Honor didn't mention Chaz and Eugenie didn't ask. She assumed Chaz was out of the picture. She sent a check and asked Honor to send her a supply of her special hand cream that she could not find in Wyoming.

Mitchell had learned that Star Lily Ranch encroached on an ancient elk, deer, and pronghorn migration corridor and that the animals now had to thread their way through a maze of towns, ranches, fences, and roads to reach their traditional summer grazing range in the Bachelors. The effect of the big log houses, each with its yapping dogs, was as pernicious as any trashy trailer park. A sense of guilt began to dye his time in the house. He could almost glimpse Condor Figg's hatred of these houses choking the passage and the old landscape, although the Figgs themselves had sold the land and their livestock fences stopped everything but the wind.

December was wretchedly cold, made worse by violent winds. When Eugenie went outside spicules of snow stung her face and rattled against her windproof jacket. The roads were treacherous, and day after day she was trapped in the house. Somehow Mitchell continued his drives in the bad weather, relishing the difficulties. The snow stopped but the wind increased. The wind exhausted her. Dry and bitterly cold wind built the snow into small private dunes on the lee side of each sage plant, polished the remaining snow into tight, glossy sculptures. The few clouds drew out as fine and long as needle threads and the wind-damaged sky showed the same chill blue as a gas flame. The wind set its teeth into the heavy log house and shook it with terrific gusts. In the early mornings it ceased for a few hours, then as the sun climbed over the aspen, it returned, brutal and avid, sweeping into the air what little loose snow remained. It never really stopped. Steadily conditions shifted into the worst winter they had yet experienced.

One afternoon she sat at the English elm table reading a new book—*Tropical Motifs in Contemporary Bath Design*—that featured ferns and orchids cascading down the walls. Mitchell was out of the house on one of his interminable drives. She noticed a flicker of movement on the slope where the Engelmann spruce grew that did not seem to be wind-driven. There it was again, something moving in the snow. She got the bird binoculars and looked. A man was crawling through the trees.

He wallowed in the snow, thrusting ever closer. She watched him from her desk, her heart beating hard and fast. She thought of the hunter she had seen in the autumn. When the man came within fifty feet of the house she expected to see him get up and come crouching forward, a knife or bow and arrow in his hands. But he threw back his head and made a ferocious face. Perhaps he even howled. His face was intensely red, and even from a distance she could see the sheen of moisture on it despite the snow and cold. He looked like a maniac. She called the sheriff's department in Antler Spring and reported a prowler, then waited, anxious and frightened. She tried to call Mitchell on his cell phone but there was no answer. There were so many dead spots he rarely turned it on. Nearly an hour went by and still no one came. She peeped out every few minutes to see if the man was still there. He was wriggling through the snow like a caterpillar, crawling toward the front of the house. When he turned the corner she could no longer see him without going outside. She thought she could hear him grunting and repeating some words. A crazy man. A horror of the situation built up in her.

Finally she saw the sheriff's patrol car cresting the long hill and behind the car a familiar black Jeep. Both vehicles pulled into the drive. She stood at the kitchen window. She could no longer see the crawling man but imagined she heard him hunching toward the door.

The driver of the sheriff's car, a uniformed fat woman with red hair, waited for the Jeep to pull up. Eleanora Figg jumped out of it spryly. Both women went to the far side of the porch, and she heard their voices.

"Upsy-daisy," someone said. The two of them shoulder-carried the man to the sheriff's car and helped him into it. Eleanora Figg leaned through the window and talked to him. The red-haired woman came to Eugenie's door.

"Skier. Busted his leg up there." She pointed to the steep slopes behind the aspen. "He was hurt," she said accusingly. "Crawled all the way here lookin for help. He could see you peekin out the window but you never open the door."

"I didn't know what he was up to," said Eugenie defensively. "He could have been—anyone. There was no way to tell what he intended. He could have been a murderer or an escaped criminal. I didn't know he was hurt."

"Well, you seen him layin there. He wasn't doin nothin bad, was he?"

"It could have been a trick," said Eugenie. The big woman said nothing, strode to her vehicle, touched Eleanora Figg on the shoulder, said something. They drove away.

Eugenie said nothing about any of this to Mitchell when he came in at dusk.

Almost from the beginning Mitchell had taken to driving deep distances through the state. He had never known such driving pleasure, clear roads empty of traffic, and on all sides the vast basin and range landscapes. He drove greasy back roads, through red canyons trickling dirt from slides, over prairie cresting in slow waves. He climbed mountains with passes open only four months of the year. He moved steadily over black ice and through white-outs, feeling the truck shake with the punching wind. Once or twice he was stranded on dirt roads made slippery as lard by rain swelling the bentonite in the soil. There was nothing to do but sit and wait until the road dried out enough for the tires to grip. And through all his driving he played the classical CDs Eugenie so much disliked, feeling the landscape through the music.

He had discovered the ideal music for these drives by accident. He and Eugenie had argued about something—an hour later he had no idea what had so irritated them. He had hastily snatched up a handful of CDs and rushed out to the truck. It was bad for both of them to be trapped in the house together all day. It had been better with Eugenie in the city when they came together at the end of the day, tired of other people, finding solace in each other's company. They enjoyed a drink and offered the brighter scraps of office gossip. Sometimes they went out to dinner, more often they ordered hot dishes in from Casserole Chef. Now there was no office gossip and he couldn't proffer his descriptions of rock mass and trembling snow. They were more and more two cranky people under each other's feet. He suspected Eugenie wanted to go back to New York, and he half-hoped she would go. Why couldn't she say it? It was impossible for him to bring up the subject. He had had enough of something, but not the place. He would stay, no matter what happened.

In this mood, one day, driving through the empty reaches west and north of Muddy Gap, he began to think about dinosaurs. They had been here in the ancient steamy swamps tearing foliage from tropical trees, kicking huge wounds in one another's bellies with claws like scimitars. Their fossilized bones and stony footprints were everywhere. In the midst of these thoughts he slipped a CD into the player without looking at it. Let it be a surprise.

A fine net of clustered organ notes sounded, mournful and slow. He did not know the music and turned up the volume to overcome the engine's hum. Without warning a gigantic bass huffing and snorting smote him. The loudness stunned him, seemed to blow a hole in his chest. The sound seemed so intensely dinosaur-like that he almost screamed. The frail wandering notes returned, then again the ghastly roars. What in the name of god was he listening to? In his mind this music, the dinosaurs, the roaring organ all merged. The power of the organ made it the correct instrument for this landscape. With shuddering flesh and electric current coursing up his spine he could hardly bear it, the perfect fit of this music to the tawny ground, the abrupt buttes, distant fan of peaks, the monstrous scale of geologic time.

At home again he tore through his CD collection looking for organ music. There wasn't much—Arvo Pärt's *Annum per annum,* the *Trivium* pieces, and a few others. He played these on his next drive and found that the Issey Miyake accordion pleats of the Ferris Mountains fit Pärt's *Mein Weg hat Gipfel und Wellentäler,* with its questing sonic waves. He experienced the most intense pleasure in being alone, in swallowing the landscape in great chunks, drowning in the heavy surf of sound, the transmutation of geology into music.

Another time, driving, he noticed a filthy yellow haze lying over the Wind River range. He stopped for gas at a tiny convenience store in the sage and asked the old man behind the counter what it was, dust maybe?

The old man, his face so warted and freckled it seemed made of gravel conglomerate, rolled his eyes. "Pollution. It's smog. Comes from that goddamn Jonah infill methane gas project. One well ever ten acres. Never seen that smog before in Wyomin. You're seein her start to die. The whoremasters got ahold a her. They got her down on her knees and any tinhorn with five bucks in his jeans comes by they put the prod pole to her and say, 'suck his dick.'"

Mitchell found the image raw and offensive and consoled himself with the belief that the old man, out in the middle of nowhere, didn't know what the yellow haze was and seized on a scapegoat.

As he drove on he let himself face the truth; that there was much more to understanding the place than driving back roads and fitting music to abrupt topography, and that he was too late. He longed to go on foot into the difficult terrain of the Absarokas, where there were still grizzlies and mountain lions, into the Beartooths, the Wind River and the Washakie ranges, into the Thoroughfare and the Yellowstone backcountry, but was defeated by his ignorance of these most unforgiving, roadless wildernesses.

In March winter briefly cracked open. The wind changed to a warm Chinook. The meadows trickled with sheets of water from melting snowdrifts. The thermometer touched seventy. Overnight this balmy weather swallowed its own tail and the temperature fell as though drop-kicked off a cliff. The next morning a black roll cloud crushed the landscape and blasted the icy prairie with billows of snow.

"Spring blizzard," said Mitchell, irritated at being housebound. He gathered up a pile of wildlife magazines and papers, touched a match to the kindling in the fireplace and settled in for a day of reading. He had become aware of the euphemisms for "killing"—harvest, put down, euthanize. He understood the wildlife of the place as well as the undisturbed country was under assault. Awful diseases were sweeping through the wild creatures—chronic wasting disease, whirling disease, mysterious die-offs teamed with loss of habitat and encroachment on ancient migration routes. He knew he was seeing the end of this wild world and time. Of course, thought Eugenie when she heard the clink of the decanter lip on his glass, he would not sit by the fire without his whiskey.

It was nearly noon when Eugenie, making a ham and cheese casserole, heard Mitchell curse. There was the sound of shattering glass, and she guessed he'd thrown or dropped his whiskey glass on the stone hearth.

"What is it?" she called.

He came shaking into the kitchen, the paper in his hand making a sound like the slats of a venetian blind in an open window.

"These *monsters!*" he said. He held the paper out to her, and she read of a teenager who, gathering decorative landscape stones with his mother and brothers, had on his ATV run a pronghorn to exhaustion, roped and dragged it for a mile behind his machine, stabbed out its eyes, cut off its testicles, and finally set his dogs on the unfortunate animal while his mother and brothers looked on, laughing.

"Oh no," said Eugenie. Mitchell looked as though he were going to vomit. Eugenie handed the paper back to him. He folded it savagely. There was the squeak of the oven door as Eugenie slid the casserole in. She turned back to Mitchell, sensing his vulnerability as a fox senses the mouse's tunnel beneath the snow.

"Go ahead," said Eugenie. "*Now* tell me how much you like it here." And with that they both knew a lever had been inserted in the crack and that it would be prised open.

She began by berating the relentless wind, the storm even then holding them prisoners, the sputtering power outages, veered to the Swift Fox store where people talked about them behind their backs. Mitchell stood silent, and she knew he was not hearing her, that he was thinking about the antelope. So she told him about the maniac crawling out of the trees.

"That was the point at which I'd had it," she said. "I'm going back. You can stay here if you like it so much. Go native. Get yourself an ATV and a gun and a knife."

"A man crawling out of the trees? He was probably lost or something. What did you do?"

"I called the stupid sheriff's office and hours later this fat woman came in the sheriff's car and that old rancher woman in her black Jeep. They got him and took him somewhere, I don't know where. Probably the hospital. The woman said he had a broken leg."

Of course, thought Mitchell, Eleanora Figg had to be there when Eugenie broke the cardinal rule of the country—that you give aid and help to a stranger, even your bitterest enemy when he is down.

"We won't be able to stay here," said Mitchell. "This is bad."

"*Stay* here? Who the hell wants to *stay* here. I have had it. Do you get that?"

"Yes," said Mitchell, wallowing through the deep snow and trees toward the open.

"I'll stay with Honor or my parents until I can find my own place. We can sell this damn house and split the money. All I want is to get out." She was pacing back and forth, the kitchen filling with the savory odor of the casserole.

"Honor will take it hard," said Mitchell, but Eugenie gave a barking laugh at the moment a knotty stick in the fireplace exploded.

"Honor? You fool, she's not even your daughter. I doubt she will, as you put it, 'take it hard.'" She reminded him then of his graduate student intern, told him about Taylor (whose name she now remembered as Tyler), about Dr. Playfire and the failed DNA match before he had his kidney transplant. Mitchell's narrow face went dirty with pain. In lying retaliation he told Eugenie that the graduate student had been only the first of many.

"Go back to New York and your job and your awful fucking parents," he said. "But I'm sorry about Honor. I love her as my daughter. I always will."

"Love? *You* don't know anything about love," said Eugenie. A sharp-shinned hawk seized a chickadee from the window bird feeder and there was a spatter of seed against the glass.

"Harvested," said Mitchell.

When the roads were clear three days later Mitchell drove her to the Cody airport, where she would get a connecting flight. He had talked on the phone every day with Honor, both of them swearing that whatever the stupid DNA tests showed, she was his daughter, he her father. She said she would come out in the summer and see him in his new place. If he had a new place by then.

As he drove slowly along the rows of the nearly full parking lot they saw a coyote loping past the cars as though looking for its vehicle. Mitchell, trying to lighten the tension, remarked that it had to be Wile E. Coyote, driving a Mini Cooper from Acme. Eugenie did not smile, but if he had mentioned semis she would have laughed.

Mitchell lugged her large bags and she dragged the smaller one, the tiny wheels making a disproportionate rumble on the rough walkway. He stayed with her in the ticket line. At the two-man security checkpoint they turned toward each other. Nearly everything had been said.

"Goodbye," said Mitchell, embracing her.

"Yes, goodbye," she said into his collar.

On the plane she looked down on the last of Wyoming, the black mountain ranges capped and splotched with snow, roads like crimped lengths of yarn from unraveled knitting. From on high it seemed human geometry had barely scratched the land. There were a few roads, an occasional dammed lake. But most of what lay below was great brown and red curves, scooped cirques, rived canyons with unsteady water in the depths, scalloped rocks whose paler layers resembled lace, eroded slopes that seemed clawed by some monstrous garden tool. On a string-like road below, the few vehicles were the size of pinheads, crawling fleas. Was this what Mitchell saw when he went on those long drives, the diminution of self, a physical reduction to a single gnat isolated from the greater swarm of gnats? The absurdity of living one's life? She thought she would ask him. But of course that did not happen, and any curiosity on the subject was buried under two new ideas—a cowboy kitchen for urban bachelors, and a kind of ranch kitchen with crossed branding irons over the raised hearth to replace the ultramodern German style.

The Contest

THERE COMES A TIME WHEN ELK TOOTH RESIDENTS NO longer take an interest in winter. Toward the end of March the count of semis tipped over by the wind fails to amuse and driving the long way around to anywhere—Angle Iron Pass is closed even in a mild winter—has become an odious chore. Elk Tooth residents can take no more of reality. They embrace fads and fancies, and fortunes ride on rash wagers.

A few years ago the idea of a beard-growing contest inflamed the male population. Too late in the season to start then, but the Pee Wee regulars signed an oath (in Guinness, for its ink-like color) to put aside their razors the next winter beginning on the day of the first snowfall. The beards would grow and there would be a prize for the longest, to be presented on the following Fourth of July. A few snowflakes drifted on September 12, and M. J. Speet, the large-animal vet, whose opinions were widely respected, declared the start of the contest.

Amanda Gribb, copying rodeo procedure (the rule of law in Elk Tooth), established a prize purse by collecting ten dollars from each contestant. The only businesses in Elk Tooth were the Elk Tooth bank, the Western Wear & Feed store, and the three bars—Pee Wee's, Muddy's Hole, and the Silvertip. Each put fifty dollars in the pot. The propane gas route man pitched in ten but said he'd forgo the chin grass. The money was stowed in a clean mason jar on the mirror shelf at Pee Wee's.

Twenty-seven contestants, from fourteen-year-old Kevin Cokendall to octogenarian Len DeBock, signed up. Kevin Cokendall's father, Wiregrass Cokendall, told the kid he didn't have the chance of a pancake in a pigsty, but Kevin was determined and bought hair restorer with his allowance to help the nascent whiskers along. The other contestants demanded that Old Man DeBock shave before the contest started, as he showed a two-inch frizz in his normal appearance. He shaved, protesting, but it seemed to the others that within days the two-inch frizz had returned. They were heartened when the whiskers seemed to stall at that length without going on to glory. Darryl Mutsch said it was because the hairs were set deep in the crevices and wrinkles of DeBock's ancient face, great furrows indicating a toothless condition. (The story was that back in the 1950s, at some branding or other, a calf had kicked out DeBock's front teeth. With the blood seeping down his chin he had picked up the teeth, rinsed them with coffee, and jammed them back into the vacant spaces. When they, and their loosened neighbors, failed he had yanked every one, cowboy style, with a pair of pliers, bracing his forehead against a gatepost for leverage. Over the years he had become an expert on culinary variations of cornmeal mush, his favorite recipe beginning "Take a quart of deer blood . . .")

The beards showed odd color and texture variations. Old Man DeBock's whiskers were short and yellow-white. Deb Sipple's, as crinkled as ramen noodles, came in black with streaks of grey down each side, and Wiregrass Cokendall showed thick and fiery red bristle in contrast to the anemic blond hairs of his son, Kevin. The Game & Fish warden, Creel Zmundzinski, also grew a red beard, no surprise as his hair all over was the orange-red the paint store called "Mandarin Sunset," a color that clashed unmercifully with his official red shirt. Hard Winter Ulph, who'd been

The Contest

born during the blizzard of 1949 in some shack south of Wamsutter, showed jet black, pencil-straight whiskers that stuck out like the spines on a hatpin cactus. A suet-faced Englishman with the chewy name of Lobett Pulvertoft Thirkill, working on Fiesta Punch's ranch for the winter, joined in and contributed a faceful of tan five-o'clock shadow. He was closely watched by Creel Zmundzinski, who knew that men with criminal pasts often took hired-man jobs on remote ranches, and that their warped inclinations found outlet in poaching and carnal knowledge of anything warm. By January the contestants' facial moss had thickened and lengthened to the point where most could scratch their fingers through the underbrush and delighted to do so. Amanda Gribb complained, for the zinc counter was sprinkled with loose hairs night after night.

"Worse'n havin a cat on the bar," she said.

Shortly after Valentine's Day it was clear that three or four men had forged ahead: Darryl Mutsch, Wiregrass Cokendall, Willy Huson (color of mashed sweet potato), and to his father's chagrin, Kevin Cokendall, whose few whiskers made up in length what they lacked in profusion.

"It's goin a be terrible a shave all this hay off," said Mutsch.

Deb Sipple, who did not like to hear references to hay, said it would be easy. "Just cut er down with scissors first, then take you a good hot shower and put on plenty shave cream and you're home."

"Best thing is go over to Lander to Thone's barbershop. He'll make it easy. Just lay back and let him get it done."

"No, best way is to go down to Saratoga or over to Thermop to them hot springs and let the waters come up to your nose, then skedaddle for the barbershop before them whiskers dries up and hardens. The sulfur in the water sort a rots the hair or at least softens it up," said Quent Stipp. "Course the best way would be to bring your razor in the hot pool but I don't believe they'd allow that."

"Rots the hair? You must a been duckin beneath the surface pretty frequent," said Al Mort, looking at Stipp's retreating hairline. "Anyhow, I ain't goin a shave nothin off. Got this far I'll go end a the rope."

Although the contest started out with jocularity, it turned cruelly competitive. Questions about beards came up which no one could answer. Amanda Gribb tired of bar arguments that beards were or were not good protection against bronchitis, that vegetarians favored beards more than creophagists, that beards inspired political radicalism. Beard talk made a change from speculation on the whereabouts of Darryl Mutsch's missing dog, Cowboy George, but none of the questions raised could be answered. Amanda, on her day off, sought out Mercedes de Silhouette, widow of Bill de Silhouette, a sheep rancher who had graduated cum laude from Princeton and over the years amassed a tremendous number of books on diverse subjects. Mercedes had inherited the sheep, the ranch, the house, and its contents, including the books.

"Oh yeah, I still got em. Sold the sheep, kept the books. I dunno why, don't hardly go in that part a the house. It's like a liberry in there. Stinks a Bill's old cigars, too. Like a ghost was in there ever night smokin cigars and readin books."

Mercedes led the way around knotty pine corners, through log-girdered passageways, into rooms of trophy heads and leather chairs, and at last into a large dim room with a northern clerestory. There were thousands of books from floor to ceiling, in shelved stacks running the length of the space. She switched on the overhead track lights to augment the natural light, and book titles sprang forth: *Saddle Galls, The Rooster Book, Into Surinam with Colonel Mascara,* and the like.

"How do you find a particular thing?" said Amanda. "Has he got them put up like at a liberry?"

"No. And that's the trouble. *He* known where the books was, but nobody else can find a damn thing. I spent days here once lookin for somethin on cowboy songs. He had the books and I knew he had em, especially the dirty ones, but find em I could not. Part a them he arranged by color. See over there? All them shelves a red ones? There's a blue section and green and after that I think he give up. No, there's mystery stories is yella, and that's the most I know."

"Well, I'm lookin for books about beards. You wouldn't happen to know if there's some a them, would you?"

"Honey, there's everthing else here."

"How did he ever get all these books?" The idea that there were shops devoted entirely to books would have astonished the Pee Wee cow crowd except for Erwin Hungate, who was a reader, his big tallow-colored face buried in a book even at the bar. Give Deb Sipple a book, she thought, and he'd probably chew the covers off.

"Well, he bought em at junk stores and on the internet, but mostly he'd get em when he went to sheep conferences in different cities? The other men'd go roosterin around, but not Bill. He'd get right at the yellow pages and find him some secondhand book dealers and then he'd go there and claw through them shelves until he'd picked out fifty or sixty he liked and have em sent up home. While he was in the hospital they kept comin, boxes and boxes a books. Over there in the corner. I never even opened them. So, I'm just goin a leave you to look, and if you find what you want you can keep it."

Amanda Gribb began with the color-coded books and discovered that most of the blue ones concerned the ocean or exploratory voyages, that green books focused on natural history or forestry. She scanned the titles, alert for the words "beard," "hair," and "mustache." After several hours she discerned some kind of order in the groupings of dusty books and she was briefly hopeful when she found something titled *Haircults*. But this was an annoying collection of photographs of American and English hairdos from the 1960s and '70s, nothing whatsoever to do with the beard. There seemed to be a conceptual separation between head hair and facial hair. At the end of the afternoon she had nothing but grimy hands.

"It feels like there ought a be somethin. I'll come back and look some more if it's all right," said Amanda to Mercedes.

"Honey, you come back much as you want. I'm real sorry you didn't find nothin."

The next afternoon when Amanda Gribb arrived at Pee Wee's to relieve owner Lewis McCusky, he said, "Mercedes de Silhouette called up. Says you come by after your shift, don't matter how late cause she sits up watchin old movies. She found what you want. I'd say go on ahead any time because I'm goin a be right here tonight watchin the game."

Mercedes de Silhouette was wearing a pair of her dead husband's pajamas and his claret-colored silk bathrobe. She smelled of bourbon.

"Come on in," she said. "I think I found you a good one. But it's hard readin. A lot a foreign language and them sideways leanin words."

"Italics?"

"Yeah. Here it is. Too bad it don't have pictures." She handed Amanda an orange book titled simply *Beards*. It was an old book, dated 1950, but she saw, opening to a page entitled "Cullinary Instructions for Christian Cannibals," that it was rich in beard history. Richard the Lion-Hearted, she read, once entertained his warriors with a feast in which the pièce de résistance featured the roasted heads of captive Saracens who had been shaved before going into the oven. Farther along she spotted a passage on beards and vegetarians.

"This is good," she said. "How did you find it?"

"It was funny. I was cleanin out that big chest in the hall and I come on some a Bill's notebooks. There was one he'd written on the cover, "Book Key." I looked in it and it was the system he used. Made me mad he didn't tell me about it before he went. Each one a them bookcases has a little number at the top, you seen that."

"I sure did."

"Well, in the notebook it tells what kind a books is in which bookcases. I looked for beards but there wasn't nothing. So I tried hair, and there was about seven books and this one. You can keep it."

Amanda placed the book in a prominent position on the bar and it was soon well-thumbed and stained with various alcohols. No one could quite understand what the author, one Reginald Reynolds, was saying as it was written in an abstruse and sarcastic style freckled with irony and untranslated Latin and French. The author also favored maze-like circumlocutions and assumed his readers possessed profound knowledge of history, literature, seafaring, religion, military strategy, dialectic, nursery rhymes, and philosophy. He was given to mossy jokes such as one about the Egyptologist who discovered a bit of wire in an excavation and declared the Egyptians had invented telegraphy, only to be aced by a rival who said that since no such piece of wire had been found in Assyrian site excavations, the Assyrians must have enjoyed wireless telegraphy. Still, the Pee Wee regulars sifted enough wheat from the chaff to make perusal of *Beards* worthwhile.

Amanda brought in a dictionary to aid Mr. Reynolds. Gradually the vocabularies of the Pee Wee's patrons swelled with such splendid words as "pogonophile," "finookery," "gnostic," "countenance," "postiche," "obelisk," "serendipity," and the stirring phrase *Floreat Barba!* Enlightenment did not emerge but curiosity flowered as they read of ancient bearded horse eaters, of a certain abbot who believed that eating too much was the cause of beards and thus explained why the American Indians, who lived on frugal diets, did not have beards. Adam, they discovered, had no beard in the Garden of Eden, the hairy growth punitively linked to the expulsion.

Wiregrass Cokendall was thrilled to find a footnote referencing a Muslim story that the devil had only one hair on his chin, though of exceeding length, and used this nugget to taunt his son, Kevin. Kevin thumbed through until he found a passage describing a civilization that killed the red-bearded men among them.

There were many examples of beards as fashion statements— metal threads worked in, dyes and gold dust, the pointed beards of Arabs, the rectilinear faux beards of the Egyptians, the curly extravagances of the Assyrians, the Hittites' square-laced beards, plaited beards, immensely long beards that could be parted and looped around the ears, but tempting as these arrangements sounded, no contestant dared sacrifice length to style. Vic Vase took up the book often and read passages aloud, mangling his way through medieval French, church Latin, and antique English.

"Jesus," said Erwin Hungate, the reader, "lay off, will you? Sound like Umberto Eco."

"Who?" said Vic.

"I know him," said Old Man DeBock. "Bert Eckle, used a work for Bob Utley. He's out in Nevada now in a home. Home for old cowboys."

Erwin Hungate lifted his hand slightly and let it drop to show it was hopeless to explain.

The beard growers combed through the Wal-Mart pharmacy in

Sack looking for unguents and lotions that would impart vigor to hair. They urged the druggist to order new improved products. Old Man DeBock, rustling through the boxes under his bed, discovered a 1946 *Real Western Stories* magazine that featured an advertisement for a device that when cranked sent mild charges of electricity through the body and was, the ad claimed, a no-fail encouragement to hair. Pictured were three men whose combined hair could have stuffed a mattress. He dug out an ancient electric blanket from his storeroom and slept with it bunched up under his chin, happy to be absorbing whisker-stimulating electric juice. Darryl Mutsch rinsed his beard in a Viagra solution, immediate results not known.

By late April most of the beards were thick and bristly. Men sat around in Pee Wee's eyeing one another's facial adornments. Darryl Mutsch was in the lead, but he had been in the lead before and then had fallen back as Willy Huson passed him by half an inch. Amanda Gribb was called on six times a day to measure someone's beard. She had a little tape measure Creel Zmundzinski once had given her. He had used it for sizing animal tracks and the trout of out-of-state fishermen. Then, two springs back, he had developed a crush on Amanda and brought her the kinds of presents that Game & Fish employees believed superior to chocolates and flowers—an untenanted hornets' nest, a wolf scat, the pelvic bone of a sharp-tail grouse, the miniature tape measure. The romance faded and died when Amanda took an interest in a fellow from Casper who had invented a lotion he called "Buckaroo Hand Cream," sparking vulgar witticisms among the ranch hand clientele.

Amanda said her friend was going to be a millionaire by the time he was thirty-five.

"Accordin to my arithmetic that ought to a happened about ten years back," said Creel meanly. He had taken to spending his afternoons in the Pee Wee, one eye nervously on the front window watching for the Game & Fish vehicles. Because of his unpopular liberal views he was a thorn in the flesh of his superiors, who plotted ways to fire him. Amanda Gribb kept a lookout as well, and when one of the department's trucks idled outside she hissed, "Go fish," and Creel ducked into the back room with its cases of empties and smelly mops.

Creel's best friend was another bachelor, Plato Bucklew, his counterpart in the Forest Service, a big, ax-headed blond often mixed up in fights and referred to as "Plate-Head" by those who found that his advocacy of roadless wilderness areas, wolves, and horse logging veered dangerously from traditional attitudes. Amanda had a warning for him, too. When she said "Sure wish I had some pistachio ice cream," she meant that a Forest Service vehicle of that color was in sight. The two troublemakers drank, hunted, fished together, and talked about the possibility of quitting their respective services and setting up a consulting business, though who would consult them and on what subjects was vague. They often spent Saturday afternoons in Creel's kitchen, Creel tying flies, Plato fashioning turkey wing-bone calls. There was another bond: both of their great-grandfathers had done time in the territorial prison at Laramie; Cephas Bucklew, a plasterer from Ohio, had stolen a horse blanket from a Cheyenne livery stable, and C. C. Alkerson, a ship's carpenter from Boston imprisoned for perjury when he tried to claim bounty money on three nonexistent wolf hides, enlivened Creel Zmundzinski's maternal lineage. But Zmundzinski's father, who wrote western love stories for true confessions magazines under his wife's name, fell afoul of a jealous rancher. Most of his story ideas came from ranch wives; one suspicious husband who found the elder Zmundzinski's attentions to his wife proof of infidelity shot him as he was fastening the ranch gate. Creel's mother died two years later of complications from breast cancer, and after a few wretched months with his mother's sister and husband in Encampment, he was sent to a boys' home and raised as an orphan.

The two friends helped each other out of tight spots, such as the time when Plato, driving through a blinding whiteout with no visibility, ran off the road and into an open burial pit for a horse Darryl Mutsch had put down and, except for the horse, which was *in situ,* put off filling the hole. The cavity was precisely the same size as a Forest Service truck. It took the two friends most of one night to get the vehicle out with a heavy-duty tripod and winch.

On this April afternoon Creel was, aside from Amanda and Old Man DeBock, the only one in the bar. He was deeply thirsty when he came in, for the state was up to its eyebrows in drought and the small lakes and ponds on the wind-clawed prairie had dried up. The wind lifted fine alkali dust from the bottoms of the dead ponds, streamers of mineral particles blowing east. Creel, his throat stinging, had driven through clouds of the stuff. Rarely had beer soothed a more parched throat.

He could see his beard in the mirror and was not displeased. It had grown in thick and had a tendency to curl under, thereby disguising its true length. He thought that when the tape measure came out on the final day he would be a front runner.

"I'll have me another," he said to Amanda, who pulled him a fresh beer and slid it skillfully down the bar. He had barely lifted the glass when the throaty guzzle of a motorcycle out front drew his attention. An overweight, elderly man got off a silver bike the size of a short-legged horse. He wore a bandanna on his head and a red silk scarf around his mouth in the classic style of stagecoach robbers. As he came into the bar he unwound the scarf and pulled off the bandanna, and Creel Zmundzinski's mouth fell open. From under the silk emerged a huge white beard that could have filled a bushel basket. It covered the man from upper lip to belt buckle and was of a snowy, radiant white that seemed backlit by a full moon. Flowing into it as twin Missouris into the Mississippi were masses of hair that on a lesser man would have been sideburns. And from crown to shoulder blade cascaded heavy, silvery waves of hair. Creel Zmundzinski slowly grasped that he was looking at a tsunami of a beard.

The stranger, ignoring Amanda Gribb's stare, called for a beer, but before he drank he removed a silver straw from his breast pocket, an accoutrement favored by maté drinkers of the pampas. Amanda Gribb nodded with approval. Too often she had been called on to measure damp beards, whiskers clotted with hardened egg yolk, residues of mustard, individual crumbs clinging to hairs like boys swinging on ropes above a swimming hole. Here was a man who cared about his beard. Its luteous glow, its fluffed fullness, the mild fragrance of rose petals that wafted from it all declared a pogonophile-*meister,* as Reginald Reynolds might have said.

Creel Zmundzinski wanted a look at the stranger's license, and he slipped out expecting it would be a Montana plate. There was a belt of eccentrics and oddballs from Cooke City to Livingston. Or maybe he would be from Nevada, a state which featured heavily bearded men everywhere except Las Vegas. This stranger would be a threat in Las Vegas for he could easily hide a full deck of cards in his facial hair. Creel was nonplussed to find identification from Rhode Island, a state he imagined the size of the Wal-Mart parking lot. The motorcycle got a second look as well—one of the new Harleys, a Softail V-Rod. Creel had been saving up for eleven years to buy a Harley, but not this water-cooled model, which he knew had to have set the bearded one back seventeen big bills. He reentered the Pee Wee shaking his head. Amanda caught his eye, and he mouthed "Rhode Island."

"Find what you were looking for?" said the stranger, and Creel realized belatedly that the man had been watching him in the bar mirror.

"Just wanted to see where you were from," mumbled Creel. He could feel his own beard withering and turned half away from the easterner.

"Since you want to know, I was born in Secaucus, New Jersey, on October 13, 1939. Name is Ralph Kaups. My father, Hayden Kaups, was a successful limnologist, and my mother, Virginia Rusling, studied batik in Borneo before the Second World War, then served as curator of Asian fabrics for the New Jersey Textile Institute. I went to Princeton, graduated summa cum laude, did my graduate work in ergonomics, married, divorced, one daughter, taught for thirty-two years at various eastern ratholes, and last week I retired. I am out here to see Mercedes de Silhouette, whose late husband was my roommate at Princeton in the sweet long ago. I plan to buy the old line camp on their place and fix it up. Moving to Elk Tooth for my retirement. That help you out?"

Creel, his ears burning, said "See you later" to Amanda and left the bar.

As he got in his truck he saw Plato Bucklew coming out of the Western Wear & Feed store with a hatbox under his arm. His bruised face and black eye showed the results of a weekend fight in a distant parking lot. Plato liked to fight.

Creel beckoned him over.

"You want a have the heart tooken out a you, go in Pee Wee's and see what's settin at the bar. There's no sense in goin along with this damn beard thing another day." But as he spoke the stranger came out of Pee Wee's and began tying his monstrous beard up in its scarves.

"Jesus," said Plato, scratching his crotch, a nervous habit he'd picked up in the army.

They stared as the man started up his V-Rod and swept away.

"He's movin a Elk Tooth," said Creel morosely. "Buyin the old line camp on the de Silhouette place." There was a considerable silence.

"You know," said Plato Bucklew, "I don't care for them new V-Rods. If I was to get a motorsickle it would be one a the old Buffalos. You ever hear a them?"

"Heard a them but never seen one. Heard they never got it off the drawin board," said Creel Zmundzinski.

"That might just be the best part of it," said his friend enigmatically.

"Take a horse, myself."

As far as they were concerned the beard contest was over.

The Wamsutter Wolf

BUDDY MILLAR WAS THE KIND OF DRIVER WHO AVOIDED traveling on a main road with other cars. This distaste for sharing the highway often took him rough-wheeling across the prairie or into a labyrinth of faded gravel tracks. Some of these roads were shortcuts, but most were long, and a few were serious bad dirt.

He had grown up thirty miles from Greybull in a hamlet without traffic lights and learned to drive at age eight on the perimeter roads of his parents' sugar beet farm.

An hour after his high school graduation Buddy's father handed him a beer and said, "Well, what's it goin a be—college or a job?"

"Job," Buddy said.

The shining light in the family was his cousin Zane, a wildlife biologist assigned to Denali National Park. He came back to Wyoming every year at Thanksgiving to see family. At thirty-eight he was still single, and Buddy, who didn't like him, thought he might be queer. He kept looking for telltale signs, but Zane was a good actor. His "area of specialty," as he called it in a supercilious tone, was wolves, although earlier he had worked with tropical fruit bats. He subjected the family to lectures on wolf behavior, wolf physiology, crimes against wolves. Every Christmas he sent cards featuring wolves leaping through the snow. Buddy's mother, during one of Zane's visits, had said something about how wonderful it was that Zane was helping preserve the balance of nature, and Zane had made a face and said the balance of nature was a dead dodo.

"Nothing is really *balanced*. Try to think of it as an ongoing poker game, say five-card draw, but everything constantly changes—the money, the card suits, the players, even the table, and every ante is affected by the weather, and you're playing in a room where the house around you is being demolished."

Buddy and his father, in sympathy for once, exchanged glances.

"Truth is," said Zane, "most of the time we don't know what we're doing. Just tinkering, is one view, another view—"

"Quit while you're ahead," said Buddy's father and silence fell on the table.

At first Buddy worked for his father, but the old man had a temper and the son had a way of saying the wrong thing. When the methane gas boom opened up he hired on as a roughneck with a crew in the Powder River basin. After a few months he gave the tool pusher some lip and was fired. He went to Denver, where he picked up an indoor job as a grouter helper. When he got laid off he took a job that Latinas usually did—making dice from precut nitric-celluloid cubes—but the volatile solvents gave him bad headaches and the tedium of drilling and painting little spots sent him back to construction.

He blamed the city for his increasing depression. He could not get used to so many people and Denver, especially Sixteenth Street, was a freak parade of half-boiled Indians in stacked jeans, women the hundred colors from charcoal to cheese. Street people swarmed everywhere, and a handful of water dipped out of Cherry Creek could not lighten the tan that went with being down and out at high altitude. There were tourists asking one another for directions. When all they found were fast food and sleazy T-shirt shops, and, down near Market Street, a demented sculpture project of metal buffalos with human knees, they got that look on their faces that said, "Why did I come here?" To this he added his own dislikes—mulletheads in suits and skinheads in waddle-shorts, waiters out on the street for a smoke break, a lesbian couple sharing a caramel apple, a black man sweating in a mink coat in the September heat, caps emblazoned Avalanches, Rockies, Broncos, people cruising, hanging out, waiting for whatever came next, all cranking along against the western flash of mountains. And there was his boss, who when he gave an order and wanted to be sure he was understood said, "You lookin at me?" For a year Buddy endured, then, after a scuffle with a trench trimmer, said the hell with it and headed north seeking out back roads.

Within a mile or two of crossing the Wyoming line it began to snow—sparse, dry flakes. The map showed a gravel road cutting west in the vicinity of Tie Siding and he watched for it. He thought he must have missed it, pulled into a ranch entrance to turn around and then saw it was the one he wanted. He could see it snaking west toward the distant Medicine Bows.

The road was rough with stiff ruts left by hunters' trucks, but passable. Despite the snow the surface was dry, and his Jeep raised a pillar of chill yellow dust that mixed with the flakes and hung in the air for minutes.

His parents pretended to be glad to see him but let him know in little ways that he was wrecking things for them. The sugar beet harvest had been good and they had set up a vacation. Now, out of the blue, here he was, Mr. Monkey Wrench.

"You want a take a cruise? Take a cruise," he said. "I'll look out for the house, cook for myself. I'll house-sit while I look for a job. Got enough money I'll buy my own groceries."

"Oh Lord, I can see it when we come back, dirty dishes, mud, dust—" his mother moaned. "And I really don't want a go on a cruise. It's your father's idea. I don't care about icebergs."

But he had convinced them and they left. It was wonderful at first, having the house to himself, and he made a big effort to keep it clean. He slid into the silence of his childhood, slept like a stone at the bottom of a lake.

About ten days after they had left, someone broke into the house and cleaned it out while he was down at the bar—took the two television sets, the kitchen appliances, including the dishwasher, his father's golf clubs, his mother's fur coat, which he had promised to put in cold storage for her, his father's coin collection. He remembered telling his mother she should bring the fur coat, that it would be cold among the icebergs, but she took her sea green anorak with the wolf fur trim that always brought approving chuckles from ranchers.

"It zips," she said. "The coat does not zip."

It had been late, after 2:00 a.m., when he lurched in and found everything tipped over or missing. He had called the police but they seemed to think he had done it himself, disposing of the stolen goods through some seedy receiver, and they changed their minds only when the mixer and the golf clubs turned up in a Casper pawnshop and the pawnshop woman shook her head at his photograph.

"The one brought the stuff in was a little guy, sort of dark-complected but not a—not a colored man. I don't know, maybe Mexican, maybe part Indian. Maybe a Arab."

That made them sit up, the idea of an Arab creeping around Wyoming, breaking into houses.

Then the coin collection and one of the television sets were found at another pawnshop in Cheyenne and the cops told him that was an indication the robbers were heading for Lincoln or Denver. Probably Denver. Denver, they said, was better for burglars; Lincoln was for bank robbers. The fur coat, the rice cooker, the dishwasher, and the other television set did not reappear, and he dreaded his parents' return.

It was as bad as he thought it would be, shouting and accusations, his hot-voiced promises to pay them back, his father shaking his head in I-told-you-so disgust.

"People just don't *do* that here," said his mother, all memory of the icebergs and the shipboard buffets crushed by the disaster. "I knew we shouldn't have gone," and there was a flick of triumph in her voice as she glanced at her husband. Buddy put down his head and prepared to weather the storm.

"They think maybe it was Iraqis," he lied. He made the mistake then of faulting his father for not carrying insurance that would have covered the loss, and the paternal volcano erupted. After an hour of shouting, his father demanding how he could possibly pay them back when he didn't even have a job, he slammed out of the house.

He drove around, cooling down, taking turns onto roads he knew too well, wishing for new territory. It had been a big mistake to come back. Things were worse than they had ever been. He couldn't stay. He'd find another place, get some lousy job, and send them like, fifty dollars a week or whatever. He'd move, he thought, to some almost gone town like Gebo, Ulm, or Merna. Remote and difficult. A new set of bad dirt roads to explore. He would not have a telephone. They wanted distance, they would get distance. But in the end it was Wamsutter, the town enjoying a methane gas boom that promised to equal the happy oil years of the '30s and '70s. The only problem was that he had arranged for his last paycheck and the balance of his savings account to be sent to his parents' address. His mother promised to forward them to him as soon as he had a mailing address.

*   *   *

Wamsutter was a desperate place, a hairline away from I-80. The first street was a strip of gas stations and convenience stores. Butted against this strip like the teeth of a comb were five or six short streets crowded with hundreds of trailers and a few houses. Fading into the desert was a second cluster of trailered streets. The entire town, he saw, was a huge trailer park, pickup trucks in front of every mobile home, license plates from Texas, Oklahoma, Louisiana, Nebraska, California, identifying the migrant gypsies of the gas and oil fields who followed the energy booms. This, he thought, was the real Wyoming—full of poor, hardworking transients, tough as nails and restless, going where the dollars grew.

The single-wide he looked at was five miles out of town, in the Red Desert, at the end of a lumpy hog-rock track. It had been advertised as "furnished" at forty dollars a month. He hated it at first sight, the scarred brown exterior, the clumsily painted sign over the door that read KING KONG, the stained sofa in the living room with its design of sea anemones and broken nutshells, the crusty carpet, which he could see someone had tried to vacuum by the flattened paths crisscrossing it. An enormous stuffed elk head took up most of the space above the sofa. He thought it would probably kill someone if it fell. In front of the sofa was a homemade coffee table with splayed legs; on it two china kittens romped beside a stamped metal ashtray dark with cigarette burns.

"See, all set to go," said the owner's daughter, Cootie, a fat woman in grimy sweatpants, flicking the wall switch. She turned on the faucet in the miniature sink and a yellow dribble appeared. The doll-size gas range produced a tiny blue flame. The wall behind the range was covered with ill-matched pieces of aluminum foil, discolored and crinkled. The bed was close beside the kitchen range, separated from it only by a food-stained wooden box. Handy, he thought, if he wanted to fry eggs without getting out of bed.

The walls were trimmed with red, white, and blue bands painted around the doorways and windows. Along the top of the kitchen wall were the painted words LOVE GOD repeated several times. Partially blocking the bathroom door was a cheap bicycle exercise machine that looked like an ironing board with pedals and mini-handlebars. In the bathroom he noticed a tiny hot water heater with a five-gallon capacity. He'd have to be quick in the shower.

On the way out Cootie mentioned the stove again. "The other burners don't work, but you can only use one at a time, anyway, right?"

He wanted to say "Wrong," but did not. Between them lay the unspoken sentence: What do you expect for forty dollars a month?

"I'll take it," he said. He would only be using it to sleep in once he found a job.

That night, rolled up in his sleeping bag, he heard the nearby yip and yodel of coyotes, but near morning, the 5:00 a.m. light milky in the windows, he heard deeper howling. Someone's dog, he supposed, and got up to start the day. He had a hundred things to do in Rawlins, the nearest town with real stores.

There was another trailer near the turnoff, obviously occupied as there was a truck in front, clothes flapping on the line. Around this structure was a moat of automotive junk, horse trailers, oil barrels, and a fiberglass boat with a hole in one side. A pile of fence posts lay half in the driveway, and tire marks veering around them showed they had been there for a long time. Pink-stemmed halogeton weeds choked the background. The owners had dogs, and he supposed they were the source of the predawn howling.

After a few days he realized there was a third single-wide

about a mile farther out in the desert. He walked to it one day, passing the hulk of an ancient truck with solid tires, faded lettering on the door that read J. O. SHEEP CO. In the distance he could hear a drill rig.

This trailer was in ruins, broken-backed because its west end had slipped off the cinder-block supports. All the windows had been shot out. He went inside. The floor groaned and moved, and something rat-like whisked into a hole near the floor. Sand-filled rags and a tiny sneaker lay under a table. No chairs. Small heaps of dried grass and hundreds of scat pellets lay everywhere. He sneezed at the strong musky smell.

"Pack rats," he said aloud. He opened cupboard doors. In the tiny bedroom a yellowed newspaper story dated 1973 was tacked to the wall. It told of several families who had bought land south of Wamsutter from a fly-by-night development company. In the story one of the buyers was quoted as saying, "This is our dream come true, to own our own ranch. We're the new pioneers." This passage had been underlined with red crayon, a line that went into the margin and attached to the words "Dad says," in the same red crayon. But, the story reported, townspeople said the "pioneers" would never make it through a single winter and no crops would grow in the desert. The accompanying photograph showed a girl about six sitting on the steps of a trailer. After a hard look Buddy thought it might be the trailer he was renting.

But it was the next-door trailer that became the focus of his attention. On his first weekend, while he was cleaning trash out from under his place, something bit him and his arm swelled to the size of a telephone pole. At the Rawlins emergency room they thought it might have been a rattlesnake and, after antivenom and tetanus shots, ordered a week's rest and no activity, no reaching under dark trailers or beds. He felt plenty sick. Recuperating, he watched his neighbors.

On sunny days a small boy play-fought with a plastic gun in the driveway while a woman in a striped shirt (the same shirt day after day) sat on the steps and smoked cigarettes. A baby crawled in the dirt. The wind blew the woman's long orange hair. She looked a little familiar, as did all fat, fair women, perhaps because that was his mother's physical type. He dubbed her "Fat Wife." During weekdays there was no vehicle in the yard until evening. In the mornings the rumble of a diesel woke him before daylight. The neighbor worked hard and long at something. On the weekends a very old Power Wagon arrived, and the driver, a huge bearded lug dressed in sagging jeans, a deerskin shirt with fringe, and a wrecked hat, disappeared inside the trailer for hours. The man (he thought of him as "Big Boy") seemed to be a bow hunter as sometimes in the afternoons he and the hardworking father of the children (this was "Old Dad") would come out and shoot arrows at a hay bale transformed to prey when they tied on a plastic deer's head. Old Dad looked familiar, too, but he couldn't say how or why. He guessed Big Boy was Old Dad's pal or maybe brother-in-law. After the shooting matches Old Dad fired up the barbecue and Big Boy cooked something on the grill. Buddy could see him turning meat with his hunting knife.

So far, so good, but then their dogs began coming around. He had a trash bag of garbage in the Jeep to drop at the dump on his next trip to town, but was disagreeably surprised one morning to see a dog leap out of the vehicle with a slice of moldy bread in its jaws. Trash, coffee grounds, bacon grease, plastic wrappers were all over the Jeep, and it took him a long time to clean the vehicle. When he was done he walked over to their trailer.

Old Dad had built a plywood entryway with three steps and a handrail. Next to the entryway was a scrap-wood lean-to with a basketball hoop on the center post, milk crates of automotive parts lined up on the ground.

Fat Wife opened the door. The smell of cigarette smoke came with her.

"Yeah?" she said, lighting another.

"Hi. I'm your neighbor—Buddy Millar. Uh—I'm having a little problem with your dogs. Dog. The brown one." Two were black and one was brown, all of indeterminate breed.

"Buddy Millar! I *knew* there was something. I told Rase you looked real familiar."

He stared at her. The frizzled red hair showed dark at the roots, and the long ends straggled across her shoulders like damp raffia, the finer strands caught in the fleece fabric of the grimy anorak she wore. Her face was so oily it seemed metaled. Behind her he could see a brown chair, the floor littered with clothing and toys.

"I'm Cheri. Cheri Bise back in high school. Cheri Wham now. Me and Rase Wham got married."

Slowly it came to him, the high school bully, Rase Wham, had dropped out in tenth grade. Wham had been a vicious sociopath. Cheri Bise, the overweight slut whose insecurity made her an easy sexual conquest, had disappeared around the same time.

"Come on in, have a cup a coffee." There was a highway of festering pimples alongside her nose. She cleared a path in the debris by kicking toys left and right. Reluctantly he went inside. It stank of cigarettes, garbage, and feces. The television set stuttered colors.

"What are you doing down here?" he asked, taking shallow breaths.

"Rase is workin for Halliburton now. He used a work for a drillin outfit but the well froze and there was a blowout and it kind a hurt him. He had a concussion. Last year. And I work Fridays in the school cafeteria."

He understood from the tone in her voice that she considered the cafeteria job a career.

"Barbette's in school, second grade, and that's Vernon Clarence—" She pointed at the dull-faced boy of four or five holding a box of Cracker Jacks. "And that's the baby, Lye." The diaper-clad baby was crawling toward them, his sticky fingers furred with lint and clutching a tiny red car that Buddy recognized as an Aston Martin. The kid, clinging to Buddy's knee, clawed himself upright and thrust the toy at him.

"Caw!" said the child.

"Yes, it's a nice car," said Buddy. In the room beyond he could see a bed heaped with grimy blankets.

"Caw!"

Cheri reheated stale coffee in a saucepan, poured the pungent liquid into mugs emblazoned GO POKES, set one before him. She did not proffer milk nor sugar. She sat down at the table and blew on her coffee.

"And we're expectin the next one in December, week before Christmas. It's hard on a kid have a birthday that close a Christmas, but you sure don't think a that when you're doin it." She had a spit-frilled way of talking.

The baby was staring at Buddy with savage intensity, as though he were going to utter a great scientific truth never before known. His face reddened and the vein in his forehead stood out. He grunted and with an explosive burst filled his diaper.

While Cheri changed him on the kitchen table less than eighteen inches from Buddy's coffee cup, he looked around to avoid watching her mop at Lye's besmeared buttocks and scrotum. On the floor several feathers were stuck in a coagulated blob. Wads of trodden gum appeared as archipelagoes in a mud-colored sea while bits of popcorn, string ends, torn paper, a crushed McDonald's cup, and candy wrappers made up the flotsam. An electric wall heater stuck out into the room. On top of it were three coffee mugs, two beer cans, several brimming ashtrays, a tiny plastic fox, and a prescription bottle. Through the amber plastic of the bottle he could see the dark forms of capsules.

There was a sudden plop as Cheri threw the loaded diaper into an open pail already seething with banana peels, coffee grounds, and prehistoric diapers.

The older child, Vernon Clarence, edged along the sofa toward the wall heater. His small hands grasped a beer can and shook it. He dropped it on the floor and tried the other, which responded with a promising slosh. He drank the dregs, warm beer running down his chin and soaking his pajama top. Buddy wondered if he should mention to Cheri that the kid was drinking beer, decided against it. The freshly emptied can rolled under the sofa.

Cheri suddenly got up, lunged for the cupboard, and retrieved a package. She shook several small bright pink cakes bristling with shredded coconut onto a chipped saucer.

"Go on! Take one!" She held the saucer in front of his face as Lye had held the toy car.

He took one. A coconut point stuck into his finger like a staple. He put the cake on the table. Lye seized it and mumbled "Caw!" as he gummed the confection. From across the room Vernon Clarence started to bawl, pointing eloquently at Lye, whose face was crowded by the pink mass.

"Here you go! Catch!" shouted Cheri, hurling a cake at the child. It hit an ashtray on the coffee table and sent butts and ash flying.

"I've got a get going," said Buddy, rising. "I just wanted to mention about the dogs—dog. And introduce myself."

"Well, I'm thrilled," said Cheri. "I always had a big crush on you in school. All the girls thought you was cute. Rase will just about pass out when I tell him who our new neighbor is." She snapped a cigarette from the package on the table.

"Say hello to him for me," said Buddy, struggling with the

door latch, which was some devious childproof design. He glanced around the room as he backed out. The fastidious Vernon Clarence was picking a cigarette butt from his confectionary prize.

Buddy's trailer seemed a cozy haven in contrast with the Whams', and he quickly made his bed and washed the dishes lest he become like them.

On the Saturday, unseasonably warm, he felt better than he had in a week and went into town for groceries—chocolate bars, pork chops, frozen French fries, frozen waffles, two bakery pies, and no vegetables. At the liquor store he bought a bottle of bourbon. As he drove past the Whams' trailer he saw them all outside, leaning over the back of Big Boy's truck, where several rigid animal legs indicated a successful hunt. Old Dad—he had to start thinking of him as Rase Wham—was wielding a bloody knife. There were two six-packs on the roof of the truck cab. Cheri, also with a knife, waved at him and he waved back.

He put his groceries away, eating one of the pies as he did so, wishing the refrigerator's freezer compartment was bigger. He had bought a newspaper and settled down with a cup of coffee to read the want ads. Truck driver, heavy equipment operator, motel clerk, framing carpenter—there was very little that suited him. He had just started on the gas field ads when someone knocked on the door.

"Come in," he said, expecting to see one of the Whams. It was Barbette, an overweight seven-year-old with sly, fox-colored eyes, her pale brown hair pulled into a ponytail. She wore jeans and a pink shirt, which had traces of blood on it.

"Dad says come over for the barbecue. Graig shot some antelopes and we're goin a have a barbecue. Mama's makin the sauce with ketchup and sugar. Dad says don't bring no beer, he got plenty." Without waiting for an answer she turned and ran back.

"O.K.," said Buddy to the door. But he would not go empty-handed. He lit the tiny oven and heated up the French fries, slipped the bourbon bottle into his jacket pocket.

The adults were half drunk when he went over and he thought Vernon Clarence was drunk as well, for the child was staggering around, sucking at a beer can. This time Buddy did mention it to Cheri, but she laughed.

"Oh, Rase lets him do it. Figures if he starts young he won't be a bad drunk when he gets up in size. It's your late starters are the bad ones. He says."

Amazing, thought Buddy. He and Rase were the same age, but Rase had made all these kids and one of them was an alcoholic even before hitting kindergarten.

Rase came slouching over, stuck out a blood-crusted hand. There was the familiar shaved bullethead, the wide neck and great swollen mounds of muscle. Rase Wham's face was scarred, and there were tattoos of barbed wire, fanged snakes, and an AK-47 spitting red bullets on his arms. His smile showed a set of broken yellow teeth.

"How the shit are ya? How'd you end up in this fuckin dump? This here's my asshole buddy, Graig. Graig Deshler. Mountain Man Deshler. He's the real thing, sleeps on the ground, tracks lions, cooks cowboy coffee."

Graig Deshler glowered at Buddy. "Fuckin bullshit," he said, but the glower was for show. He bore the traces of acne so severe that his sallow skin resembled sand drilled by a fast-moving cloudburst. But he had an air of surety that Buddy liked, and his shrewd, twinkling eyes took in everything. After he had a good swallow of the bourbon he began telling Buddy how it was.

"See, everybody tells me I was born a hunderd years too late. Hunderd fifty, more like it. I should a been a mountain man, they tell me. I'm a throwback and proud of it. I live by my wits, see? Trap, hunt, got me a little cabin, no electricity, get water from the crick. Done it all my life. Trap, hunt, got me that little cabin. Only thing different between me and the old-time mountain man is I ain't got no squaw woman. I been on the lookout for one but hell, they are all too civilized for me, just like the rest a the population, got a have that deodorant and perfume, fancy clothes and go see the hairdresser six times a week. I wouldn't touch one a them. I got a friend, he's a Northern Cheyenne, he makes these art pieces for tourists. Needs eagles' and hawks' feathers, fur. I keep him supplied. It's unlawful they say. They can kiss my butt. I never had a huntin license. Game and Fish knows better than mess with me. They give me plenty a room." His voice went on and on, rising and falling like the outboard motor of a boat circling a lake.

"So this friend a mine, the Cheyenne, I ask him once, 'You got any sisters?' Christ, he got mad. Sore as hell, he's still all fired up. All I did was ask a simple question but you might a thought I was askin him to suck my dick. I *never* paid no taxes. The U.S. Government, and that goes for the Game and Fish, can kiss my butt. Old Claude Dallas had the right idea. They come messin around your camp, shoot em. I don't pay taxes, I don't need their stinkin pensions or social security or that Medicare shit. Cut my own hair, never shaved since I were a colt but I keep my beard trimmed up. Never liked a see a woodsy man with big bushy whiskers. Catches in the willers. I was goin a run for governor last election."

He released a prolonged blast of wind, and a stench of burning tires surrounded them. Buddy wondered what in the name of the revered outlaw Claude Dallas the man had eaten—raw skunk? Graig seemed not to notice and stuck out his callused hand for the bourbon bottle.

"Now that's good stuff. I made moonshine and all kind a homemade whiskey, but I can't get it to be no good in the taste. You got a have a good whiskey barrel and all I had was a goddamn old pickle barrel. That's the one concession I make to civilization—liquor. It's hard a make and I have to say it is worth all they ask for it."

Buddy, glancing at the muddy Power Wagon, the rifle in the back window, the mountain man's stainless steel wristwatch, thought Graig made a few other concessions to civilization, and excused himself saying he had to bring his French fries in to Cheri.

In the trailer Cheri was mixing the barbecue sauce. She had dumped a large bottle of ketchup into a bowl and was stirring in brown sugar and Tabasco sauce.

"What I really need," she said, "is whiskey. About a tablespoon a whiskey makes it real smooth. But I tell you what is almost as good is cough syrup." She rummaged in the cupboard and brought out a small bottle whose contents went into the red sauce.

"And some salt. There." She dropped the raw slabs of antelope meat into the bowl and laid a newspaper across the top.

"Just let her set for half a hour or so and then Graig can cook it. He does all the cookin when he visits. He won't let nobody else even try. He's out there at that grill long as anybody wants some meat. He's a sweetheart." She lit a cigarette and got two beers from the refrigerator, passed one to him. "Let's go join the party," she said, pulling on a huge green sweater.

Cheri and Graig were talkative and half-flirting, Graig explaining what his platform would be if he ran for governor again.

"First thing I'd do is make the wolf the state animal, put the wolf on the license plate, get rid a that damn buckin bronco. People say them big Canadian greys they brought into Wyomin is not the native wolf."

Rase interrupted, spoke very loudly. "What *I'd* do," he said, "is open up Yellowstone Park for huntin. Clean the place out and get the oil and minin interests in. Could be like Alaska used a be—pay each resident a couple thousand dollars just for livin here." He let out a huge gobbling laugh, then fell silent again. His eyes wandered and he was jumpy.

Graig continued. "Anyway, they say the native wolf, the Rocky Mountain wolf, was smaller than those Canadian greys. Little bit bigger than coyotes and they didn't use to run in no packs. Solitary. It's a lot a hot air. Same animal. Everbody in the state got a opinion about wolves, mostly wrong."

"Wuf!" said Lye, rubbing the nipple of his baby bottle in the dirt.

"But if I was to be a animal that's what I'd want a be—a big grey Canadian-Wyomin wolf. I look at a wolf, I look at myself. *Owooooh!*"

"Oooow," said Lye softly.

Rase Wham sat on the picnic table jiggling his leg impatiently. When Buddy, trying to make conversation, asked him a question about his job, he only grunted. After about ten minutes he suddenly shouted at Graig: "When the hell are you goin a cook that meat?" Little Vernon Clarence, on the steps with the barrel of his toy revolver in his mouth, gave a startled jump and began to cry. Rase turned on the child.

"Shut that fuckin mouth or I'll kill you," he screamed.

"Take it easy, Rase baby," said Graig, getting up and going to the grill to see if the coals were ready. He tried for a light tone. "Don't never rile a mountain man or you'll have your hands full. Old Mountain Man Vernon Clarence there will tie you in a pretzel." He winked at the drunk and bawling child.

"You don't want a cry so loud," Graig said to him. "Them wolves'll come and eat you up. That's what they do, they eat up cryin boys, crunch their bones." Vernon Clarence cried harder.

"I'll get the meat," said Cheri, and she ran up the steps and into the trailer, hauling Vernon Clarence with her.

"Everthing I ever done," said Graig to Buddy as though all were calm, "I done because I wanted a do it. Nobody made me do nothin and nobody ever give me a medal for doin what I done. No matter what I never heard a fuckin word of appreciation from nobody. And I don't care. That's how the ball bounces, that's how the wind blows. I come over here with two nice pronghorns, cook the meat, and I *will* make the coffee. When we are ready. Cheri can't make decent coffee if you was to give her a hunderd dollars a cup. I'll make it. No matter what you do, no matter who you help, they'll step all over you, wipe their boots on you if they get the chance. But they don't affect me. I'm used a shitty people. Hell, I even like em."

"Goddamn," shouted Rase, "work all week like a dog, have to sit and starve on the weekend? Listen a a lot a hot air about wolves? Where the hell are my smokes? *Cheri!*"

"What!" she shouted from inside.

"You got my cigarettes? And bring that meat out here so Graig can get cookin!" Buddy could see the cigarette package under the picnic table. He picked it up and handed it to Rase.

"What the fuck are *you* doin with em?"

"They were under the picnic table."

"Yeah? I bet they were."

As Rase's face bunched up into a deformed squash shape, Cheri opened the door at the top of the trailer steps holding the bowl of meat and sauce, edging out, trying to keep the spring-loaded door from slamming on her heels. Partway down the steps her sweater sleeve caught on a protruding nail. The slight jerk cut a notch in her balance and she dropped the bowl, which hit the bottom step and broke into several large pieces. Sauce splattered and the meat fell in the dirt under the steps.

"This fuckin lousy mean old trailer!" she howled. "If I ever get me some money I will buy a real house somewheres, not some fuckin trailer in the sand." She turned and kicked at the door, sat on the top step, and began to cry, plump hands over her face. Behind her Vernon Clarence's tear-smeared face appeared, and he too set up a fresh howl.

Graig picked up the largest piece of the broken bowl, almost a complete half, and began piling the dirt-crusted meat into it.

"Shit," he said, "this's no biggie. Quit bawlin, Cheri. We'll just rinse this here meat off with a little beer—that will give it flavor. Throw these steaks on the fire, and the cookin will fix everthing. You won't never know they'd fell. You come huntin with me one day, and you'll see I carve my supper meat up out in the field and it got plenty dirt and leaves and hair on, but all that stuff cooks off. It is not important. The old-time mountain men knew that. Anyways, don't it say in the Bible somewheres you got a eat a peck a dirt before you die?" He shook a piece of meat, laid it in the broken crockery. "Now, Vernon Clarence, remember what I told you about them wolves that eat crybabies? You better hush that noise or they'll hear you. Them wolves just gobble crybabies like they was peppermint sticks. And they can find you easy because they can hear you cryin."

Cheri pointed at Rase. "Important a *me*. This is just the worse place I ever lived." She glared at him and he fired up.

"Worse place? How about that dump you was brought up in? And I'd like to see how you save up enough money for a house in town by passin out hot dogs at a school cafeteria one day a week. You think you got it bad, but this is *the best I can do*. I been workin since I was seventeen, supportin this family. You're dissatisfied with everthing, but you ever think a that, ever think I might a wanted a go into a different line a work than what I do? I wanted a be a high school coach, but you got a go to college for that and I been hustlin miserable jobs for *years* so I could afford a buy this goddamn trailer you piss on, support you and all these goddamn *kids*. You don't *get it* that the bad comes with the good. You don't take notice that there's a lot a guys would a walked, you bein so fuckin fat and always knocked up."

"You don't like your kids you shouldn't a made so many a them. Use a rubber once in a while and you'd have the money— and no family."

"Whyn't you get on the pill? You take the fuckin housekeepin money and buy them goddamn dumb magazines you always get. You could get birth control pills instead and not jump on *me* about kids."

At this point Buddy decided to go back to his own place and said goodbye to Graig. Rase heard him and spun around hotly.

"What the hell you doin here anyway? Come for the free dinner?" he sneered. "The dinner in the dirt? Come to mess with that fat bitch I married? Come to complain about my dogs? You keep garbage in a open vehicle you deserve dogs. You deserve a punchout, complain about it. Go get your fightin clothes on and I'll show you what you get."

"I thought you invited me. But I'll sure as hell go." And he turned and started walking back to his trailer. He heard footsteps behind him. It was Graig.

"Shit, Buddy, don't go off mad. I am about to cook them steaks and they *will* be good. Beer'll clean them off good."

He stopped and looked at the self-described mountain man. "It's not that. I lost my appetite. Some other time when Rase isn't so hot for a fight."

"Hell, he just flares up ever now and then. Ten minutes from now he'll be in a good mood, laugh and hug old Cheri. He just likes a little bit of a fight—gives him a appetite."

"There's some fights you don't take. I had my fight with Rase about ten years ago."

The Wamsutter Wolf

He had been fourteen, a strong-enough kid, sturdied up by chores, but Rase already had a man's construction, big muscled shoulders, hard arms and hands like a stonemason's. What started as a shoving scuffle became a snorting, choking fight that ended with Rase repeatedly slamming Buddy's face onto the cement sidewalk. That night, after one look at his damaged features, his father had taken him to Doc String, who said he had a broken nose and broken cheekbone. The bones in both hands were broken as well. His father wanted to call the sheriff, but Buddy pleaded nasally against this as he knew Rase would follow up with a fresh assault.

Graig was still walking beside him. "I didn't know you knowed him that long."

"We was in grade school." Buddy didn't want to talk about the Rase Wham of yesteryear.

There was a distant howl and then another from a different direction. Graig snatched at his sleeve and breathed heavily—bourbon, beer, and bad teeth. His face was golden in the late light.

"You hear that?" said Graig. "That, my friend, was a *wolf*. And it weren't so goddamn far away, neither. I never knew them to be down this far, but I sure as hell know one when I hear one. There's wolves in the Red Desert, gettin a bead on Wamsutter. We just heard the livin proof."

Buddy doubted that.

Back in his trailer he realized he had left the precious bottle of bourbon on the Whams' picnic table. There was nothing he wanted more at the moment than to get stinking drunk and pass out in his bed. Cursing, he decided to drive into town and get another, and because he didn't want to pass the Whams' trailer, where billowing clouds of smoke now rose from the barbecue, he decided to cut cross-lots over the desert, past the old pack rat trailer. He planned to circle around, pick up the new methane gas road that shot in a straight line to the county road. He figured it was about three miles cross-country to the gas road. It could be a little tricky, but he was full of adrenaline and welcomed the difficulty. There was still enough light to see what he needed to see.

Driving unknown desert terrain was dangerous, even in daylight, and with twilight close he might have trouble. Chains, a shovel, several planks, a come-along, and assorted tools, including his .30-06, were already in the back of the Jeep. He threw his heavy jacket, a gallon of water, the second pie, and a package of pork chops onto the backseat. In the glove compartment were matches and candles. If he got stranded he'd be all right. He might just park out in the desert and do his drinking there.

A few hundred yards beyond the ruined pack rat trailer he was surprised to find the faintest of trails, the barest suggestion of narrow-set wheel ruts. He thought he might be on part of the old Overland Trail or one of its many side shoots. It was almost full dusk but his headlights picked out the ghostly ruts and for now they headed in the direction he wanted. But after half a mile the ephemeral track disappeared into a deep and brushy draw and he turned north, looking for level ground. By the time he cleared the draw it was dark but a hundred yards away he could see the lights of a truck on the gas road. In ten minutes he was in Wamsutter.

The Whams' trailer was dark when he drove past it but he caught a glimpse of Graig's Power Wagon. Climbing the steps of his own place he yawned hugely, opened the door. He knew instantly something was different. There was a certain faint smell, and then a child's low whimper. He switched on the light. Vernon Clarence lay on one end of the sofa, and a blanketed lump he assumed was Lye on the other end, and on the floor, wrapped in the blankets from his bed, lay Cheri and Barbette.

"Cheri? What the hell is going on?" he said.

The woman sat up, her red hair mashed flat on one side.

"It's Rase. He got real drunk and mean like he does sometime. He hit Vernon Clarence pretty bad. I think his little arm might be broke. So Graig said he would quiet Rase down, we should come over here and wait for you. I took the blankets off your bed but you can have em back now."

"Jesus," said Buddy, sitting in a chair. He looked at his watch. Eleven forty-five. Hours to go before daylight. "You want a take Vernon Clarence to the emergency room in Rawlins? Have him looked at?"

"I don't know. He's asleep now, but he been cryin bad and he won't let me touch his arm. It does look kind a funny the way he holds it. He just cried his little self to sleep."

As if in confirmation the child whimpered again and turned his head from the light. Buddy looked at him. The boy's nose was swollen and he could see dried blood on his upper lip. He could not see the arm because the child was covered by one of his jackets. It was cold in the trailer and Cheri had helped herself to whatever coverings she could find. He lifted the jacket slowly, and the child woke, screaming. Vernon Clarence's lower left arm seemed to have an extra elbow.

"O.K.," he said. "This is not good. I'm goin a drive you to Rawlins and while they take care a the kid I'll get you all a motel room. He's hurt and this is not a good place for you to be. Rase could come over here easy and start up again. And as soon as Graig leaves I bet you that's what happens. Come on, Cheri, let's go, get the kid to a doctor." He wished now he had a cell phone.

The trip to the hospital was a nightmare, all three children crying, Cheri chain-smoking, his head ringing with bourbon and fatigue. Barbette had sat on the package of pork chops, and the cold, wet meat had set her off.

At the hospital Vernon Clarence was carried into a curtained cubicle by a tall, foreign-looking nurse. He heard Cheri tell her that Vernon Clarence had fallen down the trailer steps. There was a lot going on in the emergency room and every cubicle was full, people rushing back and forth. There were deputies and troopers leaning over people. He understood there had been a major accident on I-80. Cheri came out, and while she sat in the crowded waiting room under the pitiless glare of lights, surrounded by signs that said NO SMOKING, he went to find a motel room that could accommodate the four Whams.

At the first motel he got the details. East of Rawlins a semi had jackknifed and caused a chain reaction involving more than thirty vehicles. The highway was closed and every motel room in town was occupied. There was nothing left, and people were knocking on residents' doors asking for shelter. He would have to take Cheri and her kids back out to his trailer. He was involved in something ugly and made up his mind to move to Alaska as soon as he could get out of it.

Back at the hospital he found her standing outside the doors, smoking.

"They're not done with him. Been some kind a accident on the interstate so everthing is takin forever. They got a lot a hurt people here. Lye's fell asleep on that couch thing and Barbette too. It could be a while."

"I got bad news, too. There's no motel rooms because a the accident so I guess I will have to take you back to my place. You better be thinkin what you want a do in the mornin—I can take you to a shelter if they got that kind a thing here."

"Oh, I don't need a do that. Rase will be O.K. in the morning. He gets bad sometimes when he is drinkin, but you'll see, Graig will talk him out a the meanness and he'll be just as sweet as pie in the morning, all sorry and nice."

"Cheri, I don't want a tell you how to run your life but you got a think about the kids. He could really hurt them. Hell, he could kill them. He could kill you. He's a strong guy and drunk strong guys are dangerous."

"I guess I know Rase pretty good, better'n you, anyway. He'll be O.K. It's happened before. And Graig can handle him. He's probly got him calmed down right now."

"Jesus," he said. "So do you want me to take you back to your place?" He had the worst headache of his life and it wasn't all from bourbon.

A nurse's aide came out the door and said, "Mrs. Wham? The doctor wants a talk to you."

"I'll wait here," said Buddy as Cheri threw her cigarette down and went inside.

Cheri came out pulling her big sweater around her breasts.

"They are goin a keep him tonight. They are writin up a report says it was a possible child abuse. The cops are goin a pick Rase up and question him. I had a tell them he hit Vernon Clarence. They didn't believe he fell down the steps. Rase will be real, real mad. So I can't go back there tonight."

"When are the cops goin a pick him up?"

"Right away, maybe. Or in the mornin. They got such a lot happenin right now."

He looked at his watch. It was past one and by the time they got back to his place it would be pushing three. It looked like he was in for it.

There was only Rase's truck and Graig's old wagon in the Whams' yard.

They put Lye and Barbette on the couch. He gave Cheri his

own bed, rolled up in his sleeping bag near the door, and was asleep in minutes. He was dreaming of the waitress at the café where he'd been drinking, dreaming that she flashed different colors from a kaleidoscope of whirling cop car lights, and that she was stroking his penis, her enameled nails just tickling his pubic hair, when he felt the stroking was real and could smell Cheri, a mixture of burned meat, baby shit, and sweat. She pulled him on top of her. He wanted desperately to stop, and tried, but it had been too long, the dream was strong and his traitorous body went for the jackpot.

The sharp wind wedging under the door and some slight noise woke him. He was stiff with cold, his face pressed against the door, and for a moment did not recognize where he was until he rolled over and saw Barbette on the sofa staring at him. He sat up, the terrible night returning in big, indigestible lumps.

"Mama can't find the Sugar Puffs," the child said.

"Don't have Sugar Puffs," he croaked. His head was swimming.

"Mama, he don't have no Sugar Puffs!" the outraged girl shouted, kicking the sofa and rousing Lye, who began to cry.

He saw Cheri then, fiddling with his coffeemaker, stymied by the unfamiliar gadget. He got up, conscious of his stained, bagging underwear, which seemed made of transparent plastic wrap, seized his jeans and shirt from the floor, and went into the bathroom. As he passed her he told Cheri to leave the coffee alone, that he would make it in a minute.

The shower was a sometime thing, but he had to get the smell of the night's horrors off and was grateful for the sputtering trickle, even when the water went cold and left him gasping and shaking. He urinated in the drain.

Dressed, he went straight to the coffeemaker. Cheri was sitting at the table smoking a cigarette and drinking a soda she had found in the refrigerator.

He looked out the tiny window. There was a tumbled mass of indigo and salmon cloud in the east. The faded rabbitbrush lashed in the blustery wind and a streak of color showed where the sun would soon rise. There was no sign that the police were coming for Rase. Graig's old Power Wagon stood in its usual place. The first flakes of snow shot through the fierce air. The coffeepot quit mumbling, and he poured himself a cup of strong black, then another for Cheri. He wanted to get her moving.

"Thanks, honey," she said in an artificially sweet voice that he interpreted to mean she thought she now had some claim on him.

"Cheri," he said, "look, last night was nothin. It was a mistake. Tell the truth, you kind a raped me. Sooner you get goin the better."

She pouted for a minute, then said, "But we got a go get Vernon Clarence. They said he could be picked up any time after nine."

"Yeah? Well I suggest you go get Rase's truck and drive up to Rawlins yourself. And I sure don't see any cruisers comin for Rase."

Cheri slurped at her coffee and looked at him from under her eyelashes as though measuring. "I just said that about them pickin him up. I knew you wanted a do it with me and I did too so I just said it."

"But you told me they didn't believe you about Vernon Clarence falling down the stairs."

"Yeah, they did. They just said they'd keep him overnight and us come pick him up this mornin."

"Cheri, let's get something straight. I *didn't* want a do it with you. It was against my will." Yet he knew there had been a measure of vigorous participation motivated by vengeance against Rase.

"Could a fooled me," she said and gave him a horrible smile.

He was beginning to guess that she might be picking him to replace Rase. He literally felt his neck hair bristle.

"I want Sugar Puffs," whined Barbette.

"Then why the hell don't you go on home and get some," he snapped.

"Can I, Mama?"

"Sure. Go on over."

The child was out the door, slamming it behind her, but the catch failed and the door began to boom and swing in the wind. He got up and closed it, poured himself another cup of coffee. Out the window he could see Barbette scampering up the Wham steps just as Graig came to the door, fumbling at his crotch. The girl disappeared inside and the mountain man pissed on the ground, turned, and went back into the trailer. He was replaced by Rase, who apparently preferred fresh air to his own diaper-flavored bathroom.

"They're up over there. I think you better go home and get things back on track."

She leaned back in her chair and shot a stream of cigarette smoke at the ceiling. "He ain't goin a like it that you fucked me."

"He's not the only one don't like it," said Buddy. "Besides, you'd be dumb to say anything about that. He's got a temper—which you know. Think a your kid with the busted arm. Could be you next time. Probly will be you." He wanted nothing so much as to throw his gear in the back of the Jeep and take off for Alaska. The problem there was that his mother had not forwarded his checks amounting to several thousands and he had less than fifty dollars in his wallet and a credit card close to its maximum. He was in a bind. It was Sunday but he would drive to town, call his mother and see what was holding up the checks. First, he had to get Cheri out of here and on her way back to Rase.

"Well, you got to go back over there. You picked him, he's your husband, father a your kids. Go on over and fix things up. Get right with Mr. Wham. If you are smart keep your mouth shut about what happened. And he got any idea a comin over here to make trouble I got my .30-06 ready for him. You just let him know that. And you keep your ass over there, too. What happened last night was a big mistake and it will never happen again. I tried a help you with the hurt kid but that's where it stops. Get out a my life."

She gave a snort through her nose. "You sure don't get it about Rase. I bet he'll kill you. He won't be scared a no .30-06 in the hands somebody don't shoot much."

He knew she was right, and it made him furious. "Get out. *Now*. Get out."

She got up, leaving her still full coffee cup, and uttered the ultimate Wham riposte. "Fuck you."

She stuffed Lye under her arm, made a big deal of dropping the wetted blanket on the floor, and left, kicking the door closed with her nimble foot. As soon as she was around the corner he went out to the Jeep and got his rifle, brought it inside, and loaded it.

He watched their trailer through the scope, expecting to see Rase Wham leap down the stairs in a blind fury, coming for him. But nothing happened and he supposed Cheri had kept her mouth shut for the moment, that they were all pigging out on Sugar Puffs, even the mountain man. He stripped his bed and shoved every soiled garment and sheet and pillow slip he could find into the laundry bag ready to go into town and spend the morning at the local laundry. He'd call his mother and find out about his checks, get his cousin Zane's telephone number.

Before he could leave he saw Graig and Cheri get in the Power Wagon and drive away. He guessed they were going to pick up Vernon Clarence, who probably had quite a hangover. That left Rase alone in the trailer with Barbette and Lye. If he was going to make a move now would probably be the time.

He rushed out to his Jeep, threw the laundry in, and took the way past the pack rat trailer across the sand and sage rather than drive past Rase's trailer, where the aggrieved husband could pick him off from a window.

His own tires had left a distinct trail from the night before, and he followed them easily but drove across the shallow end of the wash rather than going completely around it. The incline was steep but not impossible. Still, a bad place to get stuck.

While his clothes were washing he called his parents' house.

"Buddy, where in the world are you?"

"Didn't you get the letter I sent with the address?"

"No. Quite a lot a mail *for* you, but nothing from you."

"Ma, I got a ask you for a favor. I need my paycheck and savins account check really bad. Kind of a difficult situation has developed here. I decided I'm probly goin a Alaska, maybe contact Zane, stay there a few days if it's all right with him, get a job on one a the fishin boats. So I need Zane's address and telephone number. So I can call him. Like I don't know if he's on the coast or what. But most of all I need those checks. Can you send them Express Mail? Or I suppose I could drive up there and get them if Dad's not still mad."

"Denali is in the middle, not on the coast. And Dad *is* still mad and as a matter a fact he's got all your mail in a big envelope out in his truck."

"Oh no." His father was capable of forging Buddy's signature and cashing the checks, taking the money against the value of the stolen goods. "But I need those checks. Can you talk to him, tell him I'm kind a desperate? Call you back tomorrow?"

"I'll try, Buddy. And I'll dig up Zane's number and address. Some place like 'Banana.' I keep it up in the attic with the Christmas card boxes."

"O.K., Ma, I'll call you tomorrow around noon. Love you."

*   *   *

He spent an uneasy night, the rifle in bed with him, half-expecting to hear Rase Wham kick in the barricaded door. Hadn't Rase said he had an AK-47? Mr. Kalashnikov's little invention could shoot through a trailer as if it were made of rotten muslin. But Monday morning came, and with it the receding rumble of Rase's truck as he drove to work in the near dark.

At noon Buddy went to town to call his mother. His father answered.

"Yes, your checks are here. I got them out in the truck. Your mother told me you were havin a problem. What kind a problem?"

There was no point trying to hide anything from his father. He told him that Rase Wham had erupted in his life again, that something had happened with the wife, that he was worried that Rase might shoot him.

"Jesus, Buddy, not *him* again. You got a real talent for trouble. Listen, you better get out a there. He could do it and maybe get away with it. His old man is Apollo Wham—Polly Wham—in the legislature now, knows everbody. He could pull strings and sweep the dirt under the rug. Just come on home right now. Don't waste time talkin on the phone, don't go pack your bags, just get in your Jeep and get here. Say it will take you five hours—get your ass home. *Now*. We'll discuss the ramifications when you get here."

It was a relief to know that his father thought the situation was serious. He was right—get out now while Rase was at work. But he didn't want to leave his clothes, the arrowhead he'd found, and the .30-06 still in the trailer. At some point he would have to go back for them.

*   *   *

At home he spent hours with his father driving around and talking. He told him everything, about the mountain man, about Rase's kids, Vernon Clarence's broken arm, the drive to the hospital, and about Cheri's successful assault.

He called Zane in Nenana, Alaska.

"Buddy, that's great! I've been trying for years to get some of the family to come on out here and look at the finest piece of real estate on the globe. I got a couple friends know some guys that fish and I'll ask around, see if there's any jobs. Even if you don't get on a boat there's some work. When do you think you'll be out?"

"Pretty soon. I got a go back to Wamsutter and get my stuff and I got a do it before the storms come. There's already been some snow. You got snow there?"

"Do birds have four toes?"

The next day, a Thursday, cold, cloudy, and packing a strong wind, he drove back to Wamsutter and took the bad dirt track out to the trailer, sliding down into the wash and clawing his way up the other side. Although he'd been gone only three days, there were two more drill rigs in sight. The weather report said possible snow showers. As he parked at the trailer a few flakes of snow fell and he could smell a storm closing in, not snow showers but a mean storm. Once again the weather report was wrong.

Nothing inside the trailer was disturbed. He went first to the little kitchen window and looked out.

There were no vehicles at the Wham trailer.

"Nobody home," he said to himself. He gathered his clothes, blankets and sheets, and his rifle, still in the bed, packed them in the Jeep. He would call Cootie and tell her that one month of trailer life in the Red Desert had been enough for him.

*　　*　　*

In Wamsutter he parked in front of the post office and, mindful of the rifle in the back, was locking the Jeep when he heard a child's voice.

"Buddy!" It was Barbette, a half-eaten apple in her hand.

"Well, well, it's the Sugar Puff girl. How are you, Barbette?"

"I'm not the Sugar Puff girl anymore. Graig says Sugar Puffs aren't no good for you. But apples and bananas and grapes are."

He looked around nervously but did not see Rase's truck. He did see Graig's old Power Wagon, and walking toward it were Cheri, holding Lye, and Graig. Vernon Clarence skipped along, singing some small song and gripping Graig's shirt fringe with his good hand.

"Mama! Graig, *lookit!*" Barbette screeched. *"It's Buddy!"*

He lifted his hand in a lukewarm salute, not knowing if Rase would come out next, his arms full of beer, his heart full of murder. Cheri gave him a canary-eating grin, and Graig rumbled and laughed.

"Son of a bitch, if it ain't old mountain man Buddy. We figured you skipped out and we'd never see you again."

"I just come back pick up my stuff at the trailer. I'm headin out, actually. Goin a—west. Heard about a job." That was in case Rase asked where he had gone. Rase was capable of following him to Alaska. Another good reason to work on a boat.

Vernon Clarence was pulling at his sleeve. He seemed a different child, the dull face animated, his eyes bright and bold.

"Buddy," he said. "Buddy. Buddy. Buddy, guess what?"

"What? I see you still got your arm in that red cast."

"Buddy." And he pulled hard. "I want a tell you somethin. A secret."

Buddy crouched down, and Vernon Clarence's sticky lips came close to his ear. He whispered loudly and happily.

"Buddy, *the wufs ate Daddy*." He laughed, paused to watch the effect this news would have. Buddy, without any effort, looked astonished. Vernon Clarence continued to unload his momentous news.

"And Graig says not to tell nobody. Graig is our daddy now. And no wufs can eat him because he is their friend! And they won't eat *us* because he is our new daddy!"

"Congratulations," he whispered back to Vernon Clarence and stood up. Something very bad had happened to Rase.

Graig was looking at him. He had to have guessed what Vernon Clarence had whispered. Buddy extended one hand helplessly as if there was nothing to say, found himself looking into the mountain man's eyes. The old merry twinkle was extinguished. A hard, alpha stare had taken its place. Cheri must have told him her version of what had happened the night Vernon Clarence's arm was broken, and Graig now saw him as a rival.

He meant to say something mollifying, add an exit line, and get the hell out of Wamsutter, but he began to back away and when he opened his mouth what he said was "I see you got your own pack now."

Summer of the Hot Tubs

Elk Tooth, Wyoming, has little going for it beyond the junkyard despite a population of nearly eighty people. If you want a fancy dinner or batteries or tampons you drive forty-four miles down Dog Ear Creek until you hit Sack and there are two stores and a garage. But Elk Tooth has its attractions—the three bars—Silvertip, the Pee Wee, and Muddy's Hole.

The old tradition of pioneer wayside eating houses—road ranches—hangs on as well. There is one of these north of town which serves supper for three dollars although there is no menu choice and Mrs. Polidora uses paper plates, unsatisfactory if you like to hear your fork clink. Paper plates or not, Mrs. Polidora will put a platter of elk steaks on the table flanked by a big green bowl of mashed potatoes, a pitcher of milk gravy, and a saucer of chokecherry jelly. Somehow she can make that elk last a year.

In Elk Tooth everyone tries to be a character and with some success. There is little more to it than being broke, proud, ingenious and setting your heels against civilized society's pull.

Mrs. Polidora's steady customer is Willy Huson, who fixes trucks and lawn mowers in a minimal way. He was born and raised in Elk Tooth but for years lived in distant cities in distant states working as a mechanic for United Airlines. When questioned why he left a lucrative job to return to Elk Tooth he says, "I couldn't take it no more." What "it" is no one asks, for everyone

Bad Dirt

in Wyoming knows of the red hell that lies beyond the state's borders. He lives with a tan dog he calls Igor.

Willy Huson has neither workshop nor garage but tinkers in the narrow dirt run in front of his trailer. If the job is a big truck he parks it in the road and lies under it after putting up a folding sign at the curve. The sign says SAND HER DOWN, which is Willy's way of saying "Go slow, mechanic in road." Igor, seeing Willy lying in the road, follows his example and has been hit twice.

Sometimes, in a burst of energy, Willy continues to work on a vehicle after the problem is repaired, putting in salvaged hoses, running wires to buttons and switches. Deb Sipple, a character himself, once drove away in his 1983 Toyota pickup with a freshly flushed radiator and eleven toggle switches on the dashboard that activated nothing. Mrs. Straw Bird got her Explorer back with an enormous fixed spotlight on top that her husband said would do very well for spotting owls at night or enemy aircraft if it hadn't been that the horn blew every time they switched on the beam. Customers pay what they feel the work is worth. Little that Willy Huson fixes runs longer than five days or fifty miles, whichever comes first, but the general feeling is that sometimes that is all you need—it will hold together long enough to get to Sack and the real garage.

At one time Willy Huson had started to build a garage onto the side of his trailer and framed out a lean-to with poles stolen from Forest Service buck fences—a pole here, another there. He nailed on four boards selected randomly from his pile of warped lumber, then quit. It is a point of pride in Elk Tooth to quit whenever and whatever needs quitting. If Willy Huson stops working on a lawn mower or skimobile or truck at a crucial time, it is the owner's tough luck. Nothing can bring him back to something he's quit.

He takes his time setting to work, and some vehicles sit in front of the trailer for months before he lifts their hoods. Bartender Amanda Gribb, who has once or twice 86'd Willy from the Pee Wee, waited seventeen weeks for her 1956 Chevrolet truck and worked up a grudge while she waited. She had taken it to him in the autumn. It was a spring day when she found a grimy postcard in her mailbox. It said, "fixed. come get it." She got a lift out to the trailer with Sven Polidora, a little drunk but on his way home seven miles west of Huson's trailer.

The truck stood forlorn with one wheel in the ditch. She called Willy's name but there was no answer. She shrugged and got into the truck. There was a note on the seat. "leave money in mailbox." She turned on the ignition first—no point in leaving money if it still didn't run—and two tremendous explosions shook the vehicle. Fire spurted out the back end of the truck. The engine died. She looked in the rearview mirror and saw dozens of small burning objects scattered on Willy Huson's grass, setting it on fire. She got out. Once she got beyond the idea of a terrorist attack the nuggets of fire looked familiar; one or two that had escaped ignition were plainly dog kibble. She scooped up the smoldering lumps with a tin can lying in the yard. She guessed that during the winter some enterprising mouse had stolen dog food from Igor's dish and packed it away in the tailpipe of the truck. She put the smoking can in Willy's mailbox along with a nickel, restarted the truck, and drove back to town trailing a stream of sparks and some coarse language.

Last summer a kind of madness swept through Elk Tooth, a passion for outdoor hot tubs. No one, of course, bought one. All of them were fashioned from scrap metal, old stock tanks, and odds and ends found at Donald's Rawhide Cowboy Junkyard. The more fastidious built plank boardwalks around the tub perimeters to keep dirt and cactus spines out of the water. In a fuel pinch, sections of the walk could be tossed into the firebox. All the hot tubs were heated by wood-fired stoves.

Willy Huson, who sets his heels not only against the outside world but against Elk Tooth's social leaders, was a holdout, full of scorn for outdoor bathing. "If I want a soak my ass I'll drive up to Thermop."

Thermopolis and its famed hot springs was 240 miles distant from Elk Tooth and clogged with tourists. A willingness to go there, said Deb Sipple, showed how Willy's mind had been damaged by out-of-state residence.

"Thing is," said Sipple, "I seen his expression when he was lookin at *my* hot tub. He'd give his left nut a have one just like it."

Near the end of the summer Willy Huson visited his grandmother on the old family ranch near Lingle, where the Husons had run cows since 1872. Foraging through an equipment shed he came across an object that screamed "hot tub." Better than "hot tub" it screamed "weird and unique hot tub unlike (and better than) any other." With the help of his uncle Doug and two of Doug's boys, Pliers and Rammy, he got it into Willy's truck. He started back to Elk Tooth singing "Wrong-Eyed Jesus" along with Jim White.

His uncle chased after him for six miles, pulled abreast, and shouted into the rushing wind, "Don't you want the tripod?"

"Hell, yes, I only got the one engine hoist and I need it a hoist engines."

Back in Elk Tooth he made some effort to put his prize in a secluded spot, but given the nature of his property, a narrow strip of ground between a sheer cliff and the road, crowded with the house trailer, the lumber piles, seven or eight defunct trucks (for parts), the four-board garage, the doghouse, a dozen dead lawn mowers, a pile of stone, another of gravel, and a single young cottonwood tree, there was no secluded spot.

"Fuck em," said Willy Huson.

He off-loaded the enormous inch-thick cast-iron pot, three feet across and last used in 1912 by some unknown biscuit hurler in the long-ago Huson fall roundup. He jimmied it into place near the cottonwood, about five feet from the road. It swayed ponderously from the massive tripod chain.

After a search Willy found two cut lengths of hose and taped them together. The tape held long enough to fill the kettle halfway, which he thought, figuring displacement, would be about right. A flotsam of mouse droppings, straw chaff, and rust particles floated to the surface. Adhering to the bottom was a crust of ninety-year-old dried son of a bitch stew. He split a few sticks of kindling, started a fire beneath the pot with a curl of tar paper, added chunk wood. Smoke rose. While he waited for the water to heat he practiced shooting at the wasps' nest in the cottonwood with his .22 pistol.

At last steam rose from the kettle. There was a heavy and peculiar smell. He raked the coals and smoking wood out from under the pot and stripped down, draping his clothes over the projecting ends of the boards in the nearby lumber pile. The remnant of the son of a bitch stew, the size of a cow pie, had loosened from the bottom and floated on top of the water. He scooped it out with his hand and sent it flying into the road. The water in the tub was plenty hot. He put in one foot, then the other. The water rose above his knees. The water was very hot but not as hot as the iron bottom of the pot, which roasted the soles of his feet. He got out, danced in the cool dirt, pulled on his boots. Now the boots were full of grit.

He felt the rim of the pot. It was warm but not searing. He decided on a different entry trajectory and lowered himself until his more tender parts hung over the water and there he paused, suspended, as Mr. and Mrs. Ulysses Bird (brother and sister-in-law of Straw Bird) drove slowly by. Mrs. Bird started to wave, looked again, thought better of it.

Ulysses Bird walked into the Pee Wee Bar and said, "Goddamn, we just seen somethin. Willy Huson got hisself a cannibal pot hot tub. He looked like a missionary was goin a get boiled." He described the tub, the closeness of it to the road, the agonized expression on Willy's face as he sat hastily in the water, Mrs. Bird's expression and exclamations as she thought of how she had almost waved.

Amanda Gribb, who was tending bar, listened closely. "Hey," she said in her loud bartender voice. "Get on back there with *this*." She opened the refrigerator and took out a package of frozen corn, a half-empty jar of maraschino cherries, foraged in the cupboard for a can of chile powder. "Drop these in his damn cannibal hot tub. If he's goin a cook hisself let's get some flavor in there. Hell, I'll come with you, shake that chile where it will do some good."

They went as quickly as they could. But Willy Huson was gone, clothes, gravelly boots, truck, and all. The pot steamed. The water was still hot, and in it floated a wasps' nest. A few puzzled wasps flew around the cottonwood tree. There were wet footprints in the dust. There was no sense in wasting the chile, corn, and cherries if Willy wasn't in his soup pot. There would probably be another time.

As they turned to leave Ulysses Straw Bird stepped on the son of a bitch stew, which, under the influence of the hot water, had metamorphosed into a black jellyfish. It clung to his boot like tar. He scraped it off with a stick, got the stick pronged into it, and held it up. It swung, glistening.

"Seems like it's fresh, whatever it is," he said. "It got the right shape but I doubt it ever come out a the south end of a cow. Looks more like a platypus' afterbirth."

Amanda Gribb suddenly took the stick from his hand and flipped the blob into the hot tub. "There, let him find *that* in his cannibal pot."

Over the weeks the drought dried up the water in the cannibal hot tub and once again the son of a bitch stew lies dormant at the bottom.

It was only last month that Willy Huson reappeared driving a 1949 Land Rover and with a non-English-speaking Tibetan girlfriend at his side, two items which earned him towering status points in the Elk Tooth eccentricity race. He didn't even glance at the cannibal pot; he had quit that.

Dump Junk

OLD LADY STIFLE, WHO DIED THIS WINTER, WAS BORN Vivian Lohoft in Shady Grove, Iowa, in 1901, married in 1915 to Maximilian Stifle of Firecracker, Fremont County, Wyoming. Her husband, Max, had passed on last year on the first warm day in January. They both were beyond the century mark; he was 102 and she was 101 when they picked up their laundry. The house was jammed with ancient and dusty junk—they saved it all—from the attic to the cellar.

It fell the lot of their two children, Christina, small and silvery in her late sixties, and "Bobcat," eighty, but still as straight as a metal fence post, to sort what was good and valuable from the junk. Bobcat's twin daughters, Patsy Snow and Wendy Dobson, both with their mother's dimpled cheeks but beginning to grey, came to help. The youngest generation, Wendy's son, Jacky, and Patsy's boy, Ringold, both strapping hulks in their twenties, agreed to haul the heavy stuff out and cart it to the dump.

"I just hope we can get that old truck started," said Bobcat.

"We'll get it going," said Jacky with the confidence of a young car thief with many successes behind him.

Neither Bobcat nor Christina had stayed in Wyoming, nor had they been in contact with each other beyond Christmas cards, so the sorting out was something of a macabre family reunion. It was also a trip into another time, a Paleozoic experience. Although

Christina and Bobcat had not seen each other for forty years, the old animosities flared up immediately. As children they had punched and fought, and Bobcat had several times choked Christina until she passed out. The name-calling was perhaps worse than the physical abuse, for he had taunted her constantly, telling her she was ugly, that she smelled bad, that she would do the world a service if she shot herself in the brain. He sometimes pointed his .22 at her and said *"POW!"* To dodge their mutual raw dislike, which rose to the top like toxic cream, Christina suggested that the women tackle the house interior and the men take care of the garage and haulage.

"If you think that's where you belong, Christina," said Bobcat with a sneer. "If you change your mind you can come out and work with the boys."

Christina said nothing.

"Look at this mess," said Bobcat, standing with Jacky and Ringold in old Max's toolshed. His father had been partial to empty boxes, nails and brads, including bent ones which he planned to someday straighten, broken tools waiting to be mended, traps of all kinds, cracked glass, dented buckets, fried electrical connectors, and cans of time-stiffened oils and lubricants. A confusion of ugly feelings roiled Bobcat's interior. Just the smell of the oily cold mess made him feel fourteen again and chastised. And yet there were odd and expensive objects in the garage, like the almost new riding mower, a beautiful table saw, and a mahogany box that, when opened, disclosed a set of antique chisels.

Sometime during the Depression his father had given up on ranching and become a shop teacher at the high school, taking dozens of clumsy boys through the intricacies of mitered joints, accurate measuring, wood burning, and wallet making. Nearly every year there had been an accident in which one or more students severed or mangled a digit. Over the years it became a weary joke to remark to any scarred or crippled person, "See you took shop with Mr. Stifle."

When he was ten Bobcat had been proud that his father was a teacher. But by the time he reached high school he was in a frenzy of embarrassment. His father was a walking joke, maimer of youth, his class a kind of ritual passage, for few escaped without cuts, nicks, serious grindings. A locally famous story had circulated for years about Edward Neacock, the son of a doctor, a wimpy boy who had been depantsed and abraded by the sander while Mr. Stifle was in the teachers' lavatory, as he very often was. The enlarged story ran that one or two boys had put something—precisely what was never specified—up Edward's rear end. Dr. Neacock had called for the participating students to be arrested and for Maximilian to be fired, but it all blew over and the Neacocks moved to California.

Shop had been a requirement and its only teacher Mr. Stifle. Bobcat had suffered and made a daily show of defiance that earned him thrashings and severe beatings. He ran away at seventeen without graduating, worked at lunch counter jobs for a year, joined the Navy in 1943, and saw action in the South Pacific. After he came back from the war he went home, clad in his new civvies, a pair of tan slacks, a polo shirt, and a decent tweed jacket.

"You look very nice," said his mother. "Like a successful businessman."

"That's what I aim to be, if I can raise the start-up money," he said and outlined his plans for starting up a religious bookstore (for he had "seen the light," as he put it, during his tour of duty). It was a surprise when his mother asked him how much he needed, and when he said two thousand dollars she smiled and said she thought she could help him out. They had said no more about it, but when he left the following day his mother handed him a manila envelope and told him not to open it until he was on the train. Inside he found two thousand dollars. But the bookstore had not made the grade, nor had the diner, the collection agency, the antiques store, though his mother supplied start-up cash for each of these ventures. He had finally given up the idea of being an independent businessman and settled in Albuquerque working for a chain of dry cleaning outlets.

"Jeez, look at this." Jacky held up a paintbrush glued to a piece of wood by a clot of old varnish.

"Toss it," said Bobcat, nodding at the waiting trash can. He said the same words more than a hundred times that morning, and by noon Jacky and Ringold had made a mountain of junk in the driveway. In between dragging the stuff out of the garage they took turns trying to start the old Chevy truck. They drank beer through the morning and were a little drunk, their bladders under strain despite frequent trips into the house, threading the way through canyons of weird saved trash to the only bathroom.

In the house Christina, Patsy, and Wendy struggled with the mass of folded paper sacks.

"There are just hundreds! Now *I* save some of the plastic bags, but these—they're all mouse droppings and dust." The paper bags stuck to one another in great chunks as though they were trying to return to their earlier incarnation as trees.

"Watch out, Aunt Christina, you can get hantavirus messing with mouse droppings."

"I'm not messing. I've got on my rubber gloves and I'm just putting these awful old sacks into a big trash bag. She must have seen she wasn't getting any use out of them after a few years, but she just kept on saving them."

"I don't think so." Patsy pulled a grocery receipt from one of the sacks on top of the pile. "Actually I think she stopped somewhere along the line. Look at the date—it's 1954. She must have stopped back then." She pulled out a sack near the bottom and found a handwritten grocery slip for a hundred pounds each of flour and sugar dated 1924. The amount paid was small as there was a notation that she had brought in six dozen fresh eggs to trade against her purchases.

"I remember those chickens," said Christina. "There were quite a few and she was very particular about them. I always believed she thought more of her chickens than her children."

"I'd feel better if we had some dust masks, handling this stuff," said Wendy, who was the fussier of Bobcat's daughters.

The old lady had gone in for jars, fabric scraps, and old clothing that might be used in a quilt, and, of course, recipes. She was a tireless clipper of recipes for Golden Raisin Hermits, Devil's Food cake, pickles, leftovers masquerading under such names as "Pigs in Potatoes" (leftover sausages and cold mashed potatoes), "Roman Holiday" (leftover spaghetti with chopped string beans), "Salmon Loaf" (canned salmon, more leftover spaghetti). For decades Vivian Stifle had pasted the recipes in notebooks, account books, novels, and books of instruction, each collection dated on the flyleaf. There were dozens of them lined up in the parlor glass-fronted bookcase. The recipes disclosed that the Stifles' diet was dominated by a sweet tooth of enormous proportions. The old lady must have used ten pounds of sugar a week on chocolate cream pie, "Filled Cookies from Oklahoma," and cream cake. She made her own maraschino cherries, too, and ketchup, the old kind of mincemeat that called for chopped beef, suet, and leftover pickle juice steeped in a crock—food that nobody now knew how to make. Still, the corporate food purveyors had been making headway, for many of the recipes featured Crisco, Borden evaporated milk, Kingsford cornstarch, and other mass-produced foodstuffs. Sometime in the 1950s she had stopped collecting recipes. The last book on the shelf was dated 1955, and there were only a few recipes pasted onto the pages of a *Reader's Digest* condensed book.

"Shame to ruin perfectly good books pasting them up with these awful old recipes." Patsy leafed through *The Improved Farmer's Record and Account Book*. A sheet of paper fell out. It was a formal application for membership in the Farm Bureau, partially filled out. The county named was Fremont, the community Firecracker, but it was neither signed nor dated, perhaps because at the bottom of the page was the reminder that the application had to be accompanied by a check for ten dollars.

"Look at that. They couldn't even afford to join the Farm Bureau. Ten dollars was a lot of money in the 1920s," said Patsy. On the back of the application form was a partial recipe for Strawberry Sunshine.

A second piece of paper was evidence that the young Stifles had been hard up in the early years of their marriage. It was a dunning letter torn halfway across, and in spiky handwriting were the words "We trust that you will not compel us to take action on this check." Below the signature were several printed paragraphs outlining the penalties for forgery, drawing checks without funds, passing fictitious bills.

"Oh," said Christina at this proof of her parents' poverty. "The poor old things."

There had never been any money for new clothes or candy. She had a dim memory of walking beside her mother a long distance down a dirt road. She must have been very young, perhaps only two or three. There in the pantry with the paper bags she could still remember the gravel hurting her bare feet. She must not have had any shoes. They came to some kind of wasteland, a draw filled with a bizarre tangle of old car parts, worn tires, rags, shifting paper. There was a nasty smell and she realized now that it must have been the local dump. Her mother descended into the debris, picking up items and dropping them again or tossing them up to where Christina waited. Something came sailing through the air to land near Christina with a hollow clop, a doll with no arms. The unfortunate toy had landed on a rock and its head showed a fresh crack that ran between the eyes from forehead to chin. Yet the hair, though dirty, was a lovely fine gold and the eyes still opened and almost closed. She had played with the doll, had loved it. Only a long time later did she connect the washed and mended clothes she and her brother wore with her mother's dump searches. She could not recall her mother actually fishing ragged garments from the odorous piles, but certainly she came away from the dump with things stuffed in her burlap sack.

Christina glanced over at the stove and saw the ancient teakettle. There it was, her inheritance. Her mother's will had left the house and land to Bobcat, and to Christina she had left the old iron teakettle, whatever house contents she wanted, the rest to be sold and the proceeds all hers. There had been an odd sentence appended to the teakettle bequest: "Less is more." How many times had she heard her mother say that? Hundreds. She was quite positive her mother had found the teakettle in the dump, a monstrously heavy old cast-iron thing that someone had probably tossed out for a shiny new aluminum model. It had been one of her mother's pet possessions, and she did not like others to use the kettle, insisting on filling it herself. Christina had not paid much attention to her mother's jealous protection of the stupid thing when she was a child and occupied with her own interests. She did remember that it had come on the scene around the same time their misfortunes eased. She dimly pictured her mother scrubbing and cleaning the kettle while she had whined about how badly she needed a new dress for the first day of school.

"We just don't have the money," her mother said. "Bring down your old blue dress and I'll sew some lace on the hem after I get the dishes done. But I wish just as much as you that you had two or three pretty new dresses."

She had brought down the blue dress, hating its childish puffed sleeves, its faded color. Miraculously, in the morning the blue dress had disappeared and in its place there had been not one but three new dresses. She remembered them vividly. One was a silky rayon, very thin pink and white stripes. It had an unusual pleated bodice and a square neckline set off by two tiny bows. Young as she was she had recognized that it had style. Another was a dark blue wool with a white piqué Peter Pan collar, a very grown-up kind of dress. The third was the one she wore most often, a cranberry red corduroy jumper with two turtleneck knit shirts, one aquamarine and one snow white.

She took the secretarial course in high school and left home when she was nineteen, the week after graduation, with the promise of a job in a lawyer's office in Cheyenne. It was 1955, she had a new purse with a hundred dollars in it. Her mother had pressed it into her hand, saying, "Take this." How she had come by such a sum Christina could not imagine. The home place still did not have electricity.

In Cheyenne she rented a dingy, cold room in a boardinghouse. The work of the lawyer's office was fussy and carried a good deal of responsibility. The lawyer often praised her thoroughness and dependability. She might have spent the rest of her life there, scrimping along, going home on weekends, living a small life, but she made a friend, Rose Clover, who also lived at the boarding-house and had her own business, the Ladyfinger Bakery. In those days Christina had masses of red-gold hair, which she wore in a chignon, hair that slid and bunched in Rose's hands. Rose had a good head for figures and a sense of adventure. Their first bond was a mutual hatred of their older brothers. Rose had suffered more than Christina, for her brother Clay, eight years older than she, had sexually assaulted her from the time she was five until she left home.

They lived for the weekends, when they went to the movies—which Rose called "the show"—and then ate a magnificent dinner at Duke's Hotel. Twice they rented bicycles and pedaled out on the prairie roads with a picnic. Rose talked about getting a car, but even an old jalopy would cost several hundred dollars and gas was twenty-nine cents a gallon so it seemed a terrible expense. Neither of them liked men, and they agreed that Cheyenne, polluted by Warren Air Force Base, was an awful place.

Christina wore the fashionable long tube skirts of the "new look" and ballet slippers, but Rose, who spent her time in the bakery, dressed in blue jeans and T-shirts that were always dusty with flour.

One Saturday they took the bus to Fort Collins in Colorado to see a foreign film at the university, Fellini's *Nights of Cabiria,* and as they were leaving the theater in a crowd of students, Rose said, "I want to go somewhere, I want to see other places in the world. Let's go on a vacation. You ever been on a vacation?"

"No. Where would we go?"

"Seattle," said Rose, who had been reading a magazine. "Or Los Angeles. Somewhere in California. See the ocean, movie stars, palm trees? We deserve a vacation. Other people go on trips, why shouldn't we? Maybe we'll go to Italy."

Weeks of discussion followed before they decided to visit both San Francisco and Los Angeles. Since they had no car nor could either drive, they would take trains and buses where possible and walk once they reached their destinations. Their first stop was Los Angeles.

Los Angeles was too much. There were palm trees, but most of what they saw reminded them of Cheyenne multiplied by a large factor. After forty-eight hours of endless walking in all directions

Bad Dirt

from the cheap but noisy Hotel of the Angels, they caught the bus for San Francisco.

"No palm trees," said Rose, "but look at those jazzy houses. What you can see, anyway," she added because the fog was coming in.

It was the first vacation of Christina's life, the first large city she had ever explored, the Pacific the first ocean she'd seen. They had had a wonderful time taking in the sights, riding on the ferries, crossing the Golden Gate Bridge, for which Rose felt a special affection as it had been finished the year she was born, eating in wonderful restaurants, sharing a bed with a sagging mattress that rolled them together in the middle.

"I wish we didn't have to go back," Christina whispered to Rose on their last night. Rose's auburn curls whisked as she turned her head.

"We don't. There's jobs all over the place here. I bet you we could go out tomorrow morning and find jobs in about ten minutes. The hard part would be finding a place to live. You want a give it a try?"

"Yes," said Christina, stepping off the diving board, allured by the thought of being on vacation for the rest of her life, of being with Rose, of sharing a place no matter how small. Rose gave her a hug and whispered, "It'll be really, really swell. And we'll have a chance to get out of the old Wyo rut. I don't want to be a baker. I don't want a marry some awful mean rancher and have to bring a covered dish to the Cow Belles meetings. I want to go to college. I want my own money and my own life—and you."

The years had slipped along like a needle passing through muslin. Rose wanted education and went to the university, then to graduate school and earned a degree in urban planning. Christina started in a department store and worked her way up to principal buyer for one of the better women's shops. She bought a car and learned to drive. Every year they enjoyed two vacations,

198

visited Mexico City, Machu Picchu, Venice, Hawaii, Sweden. Most of their trips focused on cities that Rose was eager to see. In Sydney they examined the elegant waterfront flats converted from old warehouses, they had visited Montreal for the thirtieth anniversary of Moshe Safdie's Habitat. In London, Rose deplored the city's contemporary reputation for cowboy construction, which seemed particularly brash in the company of Georgian and Palladian architectural masterpieces. Even Denver had something of interest as the old stockyards, livery stables, creameries, saddlemakers' shops, trolley barns, flophouses, and western shirt factories turned into expensive lofts.

Both of them had retired a few years ago and now traveled the country in a Hop Toad motor home, its rear decorated with a toad decal, curved lines indicating completion of the creature's robust leap.

"That's us," Rose had said pulling into a Canyon de Chelly parking lot. "Just hopping around." They bought each other bead necklaces from an Indian vendor whose wares were spread on a low rock wall above the deep canyon. Rose caught her breath at the houses high in the cliff and Christina tried to imagine climbing up and down sheer rock faces to get home. The cliff dwellers must have been the most agile of human beings. And now here she was where she had started, in a smelly little house stuffing old paper sacks into a trash bag. She hoped they could finish up everything in one day. She looked forward to the motel room and her vodka and orange juice. She would call Rose.

"But right now," she said, "I'm going to make a cup of coffee. Anybody for a nice hot cup of instant?" She had had the foresight to bring a jar with her. Both Patsy and Wendy shook their heads. Patsy was drinking a Coke, and Wendy, who was a vegetarian, preferred herbal teas.

She filled the heavy kettle at the sink, flushing out an alarmed spider. She was halfway to the range when the spattering of water caught her attention. A stream of drops fell from the kettle. She held it up and looked at it. There was a tiny hole in the bottom.

"Well for God's sake," she said. "I guess there will not be any instant after all. My great inherited teakettle has a hole. I sure wish they had invested in a microwave, but no such luck." She put the kettle in the sink and let it drain out of the damaged bottom.

"Aunt Christina?" called Wendy. "What's this?" Christina stuck her head into the pantry, where her two nieces were still struggling with the paper bags. Wendy was pointing to a box on the top shelf: ELECTRO-WORLD MICROWAVE OVEN.

"I can't believe it! Just imagine, she never even opened it. Probably been sitting there for years." She reached up and grasped the box, careful not to bring it down too quickly as it was undoubtedly covered in dust and would start a storm of sneezes. But there was no dust on the box, which looked very new. She quickly plugged the oven in and heated her water.

"Good. Now we can have hot soup later on."

Wendy was looking at the microwave. "You know," she said, "this is a really new brand. I was looking at these in Wal-Mart the other day. They're pretty new."

"It's a mystery," Christina agreed.

His parents' poverty puzzled Bobcat. The old man had had a good head for figures and a taste for mathematical problems. He had often set nasty puzzles for his children, forcing them to figure the capacity of silos, the cost per hour of operating a six-plow tractor, estimating the number of tons of hay in a given stack, finding the capacity of a watering trough, the number of nails in a pound, how many steers could fit in a boxcar. Christina, of course, the brat, had kept trying to solve the impossible calculations made more difficult by the addition of their father's extraneous and incalculable factors, such as heavy rain and deep mud, a hole in the wagon box, and variations on nail sizes from threepenny fine to tenpenny fence nails. Bobcat realized there were no solutions to the problems, that they were a kind of parental torture. And, despite his father's mathematical flair, there was never any money in the house. What had made both parents so parsimonious, so cheese paring? He supposed it was the Depression and being forced to abandon ranching for teaching shop. It occurred to him that perhaps his father had hated shop as much as the son. The big puzzle was what they had lived on for the past thirty years. Did his father have some kind of eternal teacher's pension? Did social security keep them going? Had they somehow inherited money that no one knew about? And where had his mother found the money to help him with his business starts year after year? Bobcat had never repaid a cent, and he was now intensely curious about the source of his mother's money. It was possible they had some kind of secret stash. Maybe the old man had found a valuable fossil, or his mother had won the Publisher's Sweepstakes.

"I'm going to wash these doodads," said Wendy, carrying a box of china ornaments collected around the house. "They are all pretty dusty." At the sink she sighed.

"Aunt Christina, what do you want to do with this old kettle in the sink?"

"Give it here, I'll take it out to the boys and they can take it back to the dump from whence it came." She looked out the window to the driveway, where Max's ancient truck sat. There was a tremendous pile of junk nearby, waiting to go into the bed. Jacky was trying once again to start the truck before they filled it. It made a dispirited whine and nothing more.

"You'll run the battery down," shouted Bobcat from the garage interior.

"Grandpa, it's a brand-new battery we brought with us. That ain't the problem."

"Oh, I wish they'd get it started so we could clear up this mess and get out of here," said Christina, holding the kettle away from her. At that moment the engine roared into life, billows of blue smoke bursting from the tailpipe along with a mouse's nest.

Christina caught her breath. "That was just a *little* too convenient," she said. "That's like the microwave. There's something funny going on here." Still holding the kettle, she said loudly, "I sure wish that when I looked in the refrigerator I'd find a nice vodka–orange juice. With ice." She put the kettle on the range and went to the refrigerator—her mother had always called it "the icebox"—opened the door and saw a tall cut-crystal glass sparkling with ice cubes, brimming with orange juice. There was a fresh and fragrant orange blossom perched on the frosted rim. She tasted the drink, drained the glass, closed the refrigerator door, and still holding the kettle, went out to the garage.

"Bobcat," she called.

"What? I'm busy, so make it short." He spoke to her as he always had, sharply and with annoyance.

"Oh, nothing. I won't bother you." She carried the kettle out into the driveway near the truck and said to Jacky and Ringold, "I sure wish that truck would keep running like a champion for years and years."

"You and me both," said Jacky. "Do you think we could have the truck? I mean, unless Grandma Stifle left it to somebody else?"

"I bet she would have wanted you boys to have it. But you live in different cities. How would you share it?"

Ringold said, "There's another vehicle—car or truck, I don't know what—out in the barn. Whatever it is I could have that. If it's not a total wreck."

"I didn't see anything," said Jacky. "What is it?"

"Got me. It's under a big dirty tarp. I just lifted up one corner and saw two rear flat tires."

Jacky immediately went to the barn, and Christina went back in the house, still carrying the teakettle.

Ten minutes later Jacky came back.

"So what was it?"

"Dude. Brace yourself. It's a '43 Willys Jeep. In good condition. And it's still got the rotating headlight and the side straps."

"No shit!"

"What it is." They both went to the barn and Bobcat heard ecstatic cries for some time, until he went there himself.

"I remember that Jeep," he said. "I was with Dad when he bought it after the war. War surplus. Cost him a hundred and fifty dollars. He drove it for years. Most uncomfortable vehicle ever made."

"Who cares about comfort," said Jacky. "This's a great vehicle, a collector's item."

"Collector's item?" said Bobcat, smelling money. "Valuable?"

Ringold sensed his prize could disappear. "More cool than valuable," he lied. "Probably not worth that much in dollars, but in coolness it ranks."

"They're dangerous," said Bobcat. "See that steering column? Those things went through a lot of soldiers' guts."

"I'll wear body armor when I drive it," said Ringold, asserting a claim.

"If we rent a trailer and hitch it to the back of the truck," said Jacky, "we can drive both of them back to California. Tomorrow."

"I suppose so if your mothers are all right with that."

But Patsy and Wendy objected until, after Bobcat's ten-minute harangue about Adventure, Manhood, Proving Oneself, and what Christina regarded as other masculine rot, they caved in.

*   *   *

In a kitchen drawer Wendy had found scores of menu lists for breakfast, dinner, and supper. She showed them to Christina. "Do you suppose she cooked these dishes every day?" One, headed "Wednesday Supper," read:

Cheesy Roman Roundup
Kansas Corn fritters
Jack O'Lantern cake

There were dozens of lists of the tiresome leftovers concoctions in the saved recipe books. Christina saw how it was in a flash. Her mother had cooked none of these dishes. How much easier it must have been to stand in the kitchen, her hand on the old teakettle, and order up the day's dishes much as a woman of means in an earlier time would have given her cook the menu for the day. But Christina's heart was sore at the downright awful dishes her unworldly mother had ordered. All of the menus were drawn from her hoard of recipes, the conglomerations with perky names clipped so carefully from ladies' magazines and from the backs of cans and packages. Nothing had ever seemed sadder.

Bobcat had had a prostatectomy three years earlier, and the perineal incision had cut both bundles of nerves. He had not had an erection since the operation and was still wearing diaper pads for the accompanying incontinence. Although he was glad to be alive, his condition made him irritable and short-tempered. The sight of his two grandsons, healthy and big, jumping around and talking about cars and girls and music, punished him severely. At the same time he felt pity for them, wanted to warn them that the hard years were coming with their entanglement of emotional and money problems, vexing questions about the cosmos, the hereafter, the right way of things, and then the slow, wretched betrayals of the flesh.

There was no way he could know that he would outlive both of them, that in eighteen hours the two young adventurers would die when a FedEx semi sideswiped the trailer with the Jeep and sent it and the truck rolling down a steep embankment into a dry wash. It was a bitter piece of news, delivered by the accident investigation team, that had they been wearing seat belts—nonexistent in the pre-seat-belt truck—they would likely have survived. The truck itself, except for a few dents, was unharmed and still ran.

When Christina, back with Rose, heard the awful news, she blamed Bobcat. In cold anger she picked up the old teakettle and said, "I wish my brother would fall down the stairs and break his neck."

And in Lusk, Wyoming, a retired lineman, Rich Hickey, the unknown, adulterous fruit of Max Stifle's loins from a cattle-buying trip in 1928, tripped on his trailing bathrobe belt and flew headfirst down the stairs.

The teakettle played no favorites.

Florida Rental

T HE THREE BIDSTRUP BROTHERS, TUG, BOBBY, AND June, entered the bar, their eyes going straight to Amanda Gribb, a sign, she knew, that they had bad news. The fence crew usually took their business to Muddy's Hole, so their appearance in Pee Wee's was something of an event. As they came in everyone in the bar glanced at them, but nobody stared. The patrons of Pee Wee's prided themselves on their sangfroid. They stayed cool when strangers invaded the bar, but took in every nuance of out- landish behavior and speech for later dissection. No one had blinked when five Tibetan Buddhist monks in their blood orange robes came in and ordered tea. The monks were all small and catty and gave off an aura of muscular strength like rodeo riders. After they left, Hard Winter Ulph said, "Wouldn't want a git on the wrong side a them boys." And when two boisterous black couples in an old sedan with Louisiana plates came in and asked for tequila, a request Amanda got no more than twice a year, no one said anything nor looked directly at them, but when one of the women jokingly called to Amanda, who was rummaging at the back of the shelf where she kept the rarely used bottles, "Whip it, sister!" the remark registered.

The Bidstrups were burned almost black by long exposure to the sun, eyes red from alkali dust and wind, their clothes in tatters with hundreds of rips that, over time, had puffed into small blossoms of thread. Their hands were nicked and scabbed with the short red cuts that come from working with barbwire. They wore the stoutest of boots, and one still had on his snake gaiters. The hatband of the middle brother, Bobby, was a twist of class III electric fence wire.

"Tug!" shouted rancher Bob Utley, ever the jocular ballbuster. "Looks like your wife scratched you up." The oldest Bidstrup smiled a little at the tired joke, but his eyes were fixed on Amanda.

"Three," he said. "Bud and a shot."

She set the boilermakers carefully on the bar in front of the fencers.

"Tough day?" She approached the bad news obliquely, leading them into it. They had been putting up fence for her.

"Normal. But you got yourself some neighbor."

"Figures," said Amanda. "Big corporation out a Denver. And Otis Wainwright Rench is the meanest manager in the state. So what'd he do today?"

"Last night. Fence we finished Friday?" said Bobby. "Cut last night."

Tug swallowed his whiskey and belched. "Think it was the guy works for Howard, Brick something. Looks to me like he done time, all them tattoos. You must a had three hundred Triple J cows on your place."

Bobby put his oar in again. "And them cows are wild. Like they are circus cows or whatever, can jump and run like deer, swim like fish, even the calves. Them cows show no mercy."

The youngest brother, June, as usual said nothing.

A few years earlier June Bidstrup's photograph had appeared on the cover of *Western Cowboy*. He was a rider in the reenactment of an old trail drive. A secretary at the Guy March Talent Agency in Los Angeles, which specialized in raw western talent, saw the picture of the trim, twenty-year-old June togged out in shotgun chaps, a calfskin vest, and an azure wild rag that picked up the color of his eyes; she caught her breath and showed the cover to Guy March, who immediately saw a new Robert Redford. He drove out to Elk Tooth himself and persuaded June his fortune was waiting in Hollywood.

June, who had never known he was good-looking, said he guessed he'd give it a try. But, once June was on the west coast, Guy March could see his tough little prize did not entirely fit the current ideal of masculine beauty: June's mouth was too thin. Like all the Bidstrups he had a small, nearly lipless mouth that did well enough for eating, talking, and an occasional half smile. Guy March said there was a great role coming up in a movie based on the Johnson County War but with a new angle—rather than a protest against big rancher greed and dominance, a tornado would force the homesteaders' revolt. The part of the young homesteader who gets wiped out by the tornado, loses his family, and turns bad, he said, was perfect for June. He persuaded him that collagen injections would give him the right kind of mouth to cinch the part. So sure of this was he, said Guy March, that he would pay for the procedure himself. The results were unfortunate. The youngest Bidstrup ended up with a mouth that resembled two short night crawlers jockeying for position on his face, which now appeared pouty and deformed. In a few months he was back in Elk Tooth, fence building with his brothers, rarely speaking, avoiding mirrors, and as shy as a spanked cat.

"We chased most a them back across the crick," said Tug. "But they trashed your garden pretty good. We didn't get them all. There's still some there."

Amanda poured a new round. Her hand trembled a little from the weight of the bottle.

"Worst of it is," said Tug, "Rench offered us a big job on the Fishhooks. We'd make enough workin for him to carry us right into next year."

"Oh God," said Amanda, overcome.

*   *   *

Elk Tooth lies high in the Dog Ear Creek valley, on the west slope of the Angle Iron range. Forty miles down the valley is the larger town of Sack, with its Wal-Mart superstore that draws in what little money makes it to the region, with one exception. The three Elk Tooth bars are superior to any in Sack and attract a profitable clientele, some coming from as far away as Big Piney and even Thermop. Of the three bars Pee Wee's, with its nineteenth-century atmosphere of beer, manure, whiskey, sweaty hatbands, a hot stove, dusty rafters, and a kind of incense falsely labeled Dwarf Pine that bartender Amanda Gribb burned, was the most popular. The other bars, Muddy's Hole and the Silvertip, had their dependable regulars, but Pee Wee's drew the crowds.

Amanda Gribb had been tending bar at Pee Wee's for eight years. She lived in a single-wide she had fixed up, set on a quarter section, once part of the big Gribb ranch that broke up in the 1960s. She had a garden, a sickly apple tree she kept alive with buckets of water from Dog Ear Creek, a fairly sizable stream that would have been called a river anywhere else in the state. Amanda Gribb, surrounded by ranches and the beef mentality, was a secret vegetarian with a strong dislike for cows. Her own mother, who still ran a few, did not guess. The calendar that hung beside the cash register at Pee Wee's constantly irked with its glossy photos of cattle breeds. On her days off Amanda was very happy in the garden working her rows of tomatoes and snap beans. The air, rolling down from the granite notch of Angle Iron Pass, tasted clean and flinty after the body odors and smoke of the Pee Wee.

The land on the other side of Dog Ear Creek had belonged to Frank Frink of the Red Crayon ranch, but Frink had sold out the year before to a corporation that ran their ranching investments as the J J J Ranches with holdings in Texas, California, Montana,

New Mexico, and Wyoming. Locally they were called the Triple J or the Fishhooks. The manager, Otis Wainwright Rench, was an ectomorph with great black circles around his eyes, as though perpetually recovering from a double shiner. Rench was dedicated to the bottom line, and his hands followed his lead, even when it meant turning the Triple J cows onto other people's land by leaving gates open or cutting a little wire. As the J J J land was heavily overgrazed sagebrush and greasewood, Amanda Gribb's grassy quarter section was a prize worth any rumpus. And because Amanda was a woman, Rench and his men held her in contempt and did not expect any serious resistance beyond a few hen squawks. For her part, Amanda decided to poison Rench or any of his ex-con hands if they came into Pee Wee's and ordered a drink. This was not likely, for the Fishhooks gang patronized Muddy's Hole or drank in the squalid solitude of their trucks.

It was past midnight when Amanda Gribb got home. She parked in front of her trailer and got out, stepping into a fresh cow pie. Something lumbered and moved at the corner of the trailer. She turned on the porch light and saw five black baldies, the remains of her precious peony plant dangling from the jaws of the closest one. She seized the broom and ran shrieking at them, and they turned and strolled into the darkness, leaving her with a turned ankle and a bad temper.

In the first light of morning she got a full look at the ruined garden, pocked with huge hoofprints that had mashed the young tomato plants into paste, torn the plastic watering pipes. The apple tree had snapped and was trodden into stringy fibers. Almost nothing could be salvaged. She chased cows all the early morning, limping because of her painful ankle, cursing the cows that, as soon as they forded the creek, turned back from their barren home acres and headed once again for Amanda's place. She knew they could be back through new nighttime cuts in the fence. When she had driven the last cow across the creek she sat on the top step of her trailer and looked at the mess. She had found a gap in the fence, the cut ends of the wire winking brightly. But at eight a plume of dust advancing along the road brought relief. It was the Bidstrup brothers.

"I thought you was workin for Fishhooks?"

"We told him no. Plenty a work around. We don't need his." In ten minutes the cut fence was mended. Tug stood on the trailer-house steps and called to Amanda, who was inside, getting ready for work.

"Manda? I heard about a possible deal, if you can swing it. Guy over in Wheatland got some five-foot chain-link fence he could let go on a deal. I don't know how much. But it might slow down them fence cutters. Chain-link is pretty gnarly. I got a phone number, you want a call the guy. Me and the boys could pick it up for you if that works out."

She wrote down the number and headed for Pee Wee's. What the Bidstrup brothers didn't know was that she was scraping the bottom of her bank account and unless the price of the chain-link was virtually nothing it wasn't going to fly. Still she called and got the owner of the fencing, who said he had fifteen hundred feet of the stuff and wanted three thousand for it. It might as well have been three million.

That night several hundred Triple J cows surged onto Amanda's place. She wakened to something shaking the single-wide—not an earthquake but cows rubbing their itches on the corners, cows swaggering in their own manure, scuffing bare dirt. One big ginger cow had a way of scraping her hooves as though whetting them. Chasing them with a broom was futile. The cows dodged and spun as though playing a wonderful game. In frustration she got her old plaid umbrella, unused for the five years of drought, walked slowly toward the ginger cow with crafty, wet-chestnut eyes, and when she was five feet away, the cow's attention deeply fixed, she popped the umbrella open with a screech and a lunge.

Florida Rental

The startled cow leapt into the air and ran, but in half an hour they were all bored with the umbrella. On her way to work Amanda detoured to Sack and picked up fifty bottle rockets at the fireworks kiosk. The next morning the cows were treated to a barrage and most of them ran into the creek, but some stood their ground and those who had run took heart and returned, flinching only when Amanda scored direct hits—truly devil cows.

It seemed trouble never came evenly spaced out. Now, despite her protests that she didn't want to work in a sports bar, Pee Wee's owner, Lewis McCusky, donated the bar's soundless old black-and-white television to the volunteer fire department fund-raiser and brought in an enormous color set. He mounted it over the cash register. He said he had subscribed to a satellite service and they would be able to get more than a hundred stations.

"Hundred stations a junk," said Amanda. "Hundred stations a football."

This was not the first big bar television set in Elk Tooth. The Silvertip had had a monster flat-profile television for more than a year, but the only time the owners, Jacques and Martine Rondelle, who had somehow strayed from Quebec to Elk Tooth, turned it on were for hockey games and French bicycle races. It was the only bar in Wyoming where one could watch the Tour de France. Erwin Hungate actually abandoned Pee Wee's the entire month of July to follow the great race. For weeks afterward his conversation flourished with Frenchy words and references to l'Alpe d'Huez and the Galibier and other places unknown to anyone in Elk Tooth. Willy Huson, who looked in once or twice, was disgusted. "They keep talkin about the 'pelican,' which I don't get."

But it was a program on the new television that gave Amanda her great idea. She called her mother straight from the bar.

"Ma, don't we got some cousins or somethin in Florida?"

"Uh-huh, my sister Nina runs a little hotel near Key West. Why?"

215

"I don't know, just thought I might take a vacation to Florida, maybe look them up."

"That's a wonderful idea. When do you want a go? I need a get out a here for a week myself. It would be nice seein Nina again and I bet she'd put us up for nothin."

"Oh, well, I was just thinkin about it. I can't actually afford a go." She did not want to go to Florida with her mother. "But just in case I could do it next year, what's their address? And is she married and got kids and all?"

"She married a man got a ice cream shop there. There's a lot a tourists and it is hot so there's quite a bit a money in ice cream. And they've got three children, all grown now, a course. The oldest is Walter, sells insurance, and then was Marni, lives in Fort Lauderdale. I can't recall the name of the youngest one, the one that was always in trouble. I'll think of it."

She called back later to say that the youngest one was Don and he was a heavy equipment operator, still single but staying out of trouble. She had telephone numbers for all of them and said her sister was thrilled to think they would visit next year—they could certainly stay at the little hotel gratis. "That's what she said, 'gratis.' It means 'for free.'"

Amanda called her Florida cousin Don, who sounded the most interesting, on the weekend, introduced herself, described Elk Tooth, her problem with the Fishhooks cows, and told him her idea. He laughed, said it could be done, that transportation would be the expensive part but that he would ask around and see if any truckers—he knew two or three truckers who were on the grapevine—were coming out her way. Something, maybe, could be worked out.

He called back that night. "I was surprised," he said, "how easy it turned out to be. There is actually a shipment of related items going to Calgary and the driver says he can cut through Wyoming if you can meet him someplace so he don't lose too much time. Says how about the truck stop at—don't know how to pronounce it, G-I-L-L-E-T-T-E?"

"Jillette," said Amanda. "Like Jack and Jill went up the hill."

"He says there's a big Truck Heaven there. Says he can be there Sunday night around ten-thirty. His rig's a big stainless and jewel-tone iridescent purple Peterbilt, says 'Redhill Bio Transport' on the side, picture a dolphins. He probably expects a little sweetening, say a hundred or so."

"I'll be there," said Amanda, thinking frantically how she could get Sunday night off. Lewis McCusky would not like it.

But he did like it. One of the volunteer firemen had a new DVD featuring remastered classic football games of the 1950s, grainy old black-and-white films that Lewis wanted badly to see. The new television set had come with a disk player. A closed-door night without Amanda to distract by constantly wiping down the bar and tables would be nice. A guys' night out. He called his fire department cronies, then dialed Patty's Perky Pizza in Sack and ordered twelve pepperoni and onion for the orgy, no delivery, somebody would pick up the pies.

It was a long way to Gillette, a six-hour drive of back roads and mountain passes before she hit I-90 in Buffalo. She had cleaned out the back of her pickup and, thinking of her cargo, put on the camper top to reduce windchill. She pulled into Truck Heaven at nine, went inside, and ate the day's special, a huge platter of French fries flanked by fried catfish, lemon wedges, and a plastic packet of mayonnaise mixed with relish masquerading as tartar sauce. The place was crowded with truckers swilling coffee and eating pie. Amanda ordered pie too, lemon meringue, which tasted like tartar sauce with sugar.

A little after ten the Redhill Bio Transport pulled into the big rig parking lot in the back. The driver, an elderly man with curly mustachios, jumped out.

"Miz Gribb?"

"Yep. Call me Amanda. Preciate your doin this."

"Happy to help. That your truck?" He looked disapprovingly at her pickup. "Hope it's big enough. Two good-sized boxes. You got somebody can help me unload them?"

"Me," said Amanda, flexing her biceps.

But the first box was very heavy and after a severe struggle not to drop it, the truck driver, who said his name was Neal, excused himself, went into the restaurant, and came out with two gorillas in cowboy boots. In less than a minute both boxes were in her truck, lashed fast with heavy rope. Amanda gave each of the helpers a ten and to Neal she gave the hundred-dollar bill rolled up into a little cylinder. Her bank account was flat until payday.

She drove back to Elk Tooth very slowly, easing the truck along. The deer were bad on the road in the early morning when it was too dark to turn off the headlights, but not dark enough for them to be effective.

She could see only two cows when she pulled into her own driveway, but across the stream the herd was gathering for an assault. She tugged at the top box in the pickup but couldn't move it. The ginger cow stood on the far bank rolling her head around as though limbering up with yoga exercises. Amanda stopped straining at the boxes, ran into her single-wide, and dialed an old, familiar number from two years earlier when she and Creel Zmundzinski had been going out.

"Move some boxes? Amanda, it's six oh four a.m. I'm not up. I'm not awake. I haven't had any coffee, I'm not dressed—you got two *what*? This I got a see. I'm on my way. Make some coffee."

The two boxes lay side by side in the sharp Wyoming morning. Amanda with a nail puller and Creel with a claw hammer removed the last nails from the ends of the boxes and drew out the long and heavy canvas bags. They dragged the bags to the edge of Dog Ear Creek. The ginger cow, her calf, and black minions were drawn up in a phalanx, wading into the creek.

"Untie your bag," said Amanda in a low, tense voice. Almost simultaneously two long snouts emerged from the canvas bags and the first alligators to swim in Wyoming waters in thousands of years plunged into the creek and headed for the ginger cow, ripples veeing out from their armored sides.

"Man, look at that," said Creel.

The long ride from Florida had pitched the reptiles' appetites to the extreme. Although the ginger cow had never seen an alligator before, the sight and smell of these two awakened some deep atavistic terror. These were no umbrellas! She turned and swam for home, raced up the bank, and burst through the Fishhooks fence like a locomotive.

"Whip it, sister!" screamed Amanda.

"Jeez," said Creel, almost falling in love with her all over again, "that was worth gettin waked up for. But what about when winter comes? Bring them in your trailer house?"

She laughed. "These are *rental* alligators. They go back to Florida in September. I got a trucker acquaintance who's goin a pick them up. Ready for coffee?"